Saving Brielle

*A LOVE'S DEFENDER ROMANTIC
SUSPENSE NOVEL*

FAITH HART

Other Works by Faith Hart:

<u>Another Try Novellas</u>

<u>Never Say Sorry</u>
<u>Save Me a Dance</u>
<u>Falling into Place</u>
<u>Love Notes</u>
<u>Read My Lips</u>
<u>Out of the Blue</u>
<u>One Last Try</u>

Writing as D. F. Hart:

The Vital Secrets Series
(mystery/suspense)

***

One Last Gift – An Anthology by James N. Richardson

(D.F. Hart, Editor & Publisher)

COPYRIGHT

Custom Cover Design commissioned for Faith Hart by:
Rocking Book Covers

Published 2022 by 2 Of Harts Publishing
www.2Ofharts.com

ACKNOWLEDGEMENTS

To my readers, who I hope enjoy the journey of reading this as much as I enjoyed writing it!

With Affection,

Faith Hart

Saving Brielle
Love's Defenders – Book One

<u>Brielle Cerver</u> - The consummate career woman who has purposely put work first to avoid any further risk of heartbreak. But when a disturbing turn of events threatens both her livelihood and her safety, she finds herself inexplicably drawn to the man hired to protect her.

<u>Allen Jones</u> – The handsome security consultant who, after a devastating loss, has *also* made work his life's passion – until he meets Brielle and discovers his priorities have shifted.

Can they move past their tragic histories to build a lasting love together? And can Allen find and stop Brielle's stalker before he exacts the ultimate revenge?

CHAPTER ONE
Brielle

"I *seriously* do not have enough wine stocked up to deal with this right now," I mutter under my breath as I wait for the seller's realtor to come back on the line.

There has been a snag – again – with the closing schedule, and my buyers have officially moved past irritated into upset. When they called on my drive home, I had done my best to soothe their frazzled nerves, promising not to rest until this latest (and hopefully final) hurdle to home ownership was cleared.

Now I am sitting behind my desk in my home office instead of in my garden tub, where I long to be, because the seller's agent has... misrepresented some things.

That's putting it mildly, my sarcastic wit observes.

I have earned a stellar reputation as one of the best realtors in the state of Texas - and with good reason. I've spent the last twelve years making sure my clients are treated like family; I have chosen to focus on quality of service over quantity of closings, and as a result have not had to advertise in a long time. Every single client I have worked with in at least the past five years has been a referral from a previous one.

So, when I find myself tending to clients who become unduly stressed due to someone else's negligence – *or greed, or just stupidity, this one could really go several different ways* – it angers me to my core.

"Ms. Cerver?" the young woman says, a tremor in her voice, and I instinctively know.

Not malicious, a rookie mistake.

"I'm so sorry... you're absolutely right. I transposed a really important number."

"And you'll be correcting and resubmitting to the title company?"

"Yes, ma'am, it will be in their hands in the morning."

"Thank you, Miss Carmichael. If you would be so kind as to also email me a copy of the correction for my clients, that would be most helpful."

"Yes, ma'am, I'll send it to you in the next few minutes."

I gracefully disconnect the call and sigh.

***

An hour and three calls later, I sink gratefully into my garden tub at last with a glass of chilled Moscato in hand, willing away the remnants of another long day on my feet.

Stupid high heels... those things are straight from the devil... why couldn't I have chosen a career that allows for tennis shoes?

Down the hall I can hear my cell phone chirping, and I sigh again.

Gonna have to keep, I decide. *It can wait thirty minutes, whatever it is.*

I sip and soak until the water is lukewarm, then pull the plug and step out of the bath, feeling loose and sleepy. I towel off, wrap up in my favorite robe, and pad on bare feet back through the living room toward the kitchen to put together a light meal.

Four new voicemail notifications greet me when I glance at my phone, and I reluctantly pick it up to listen to them while I pull together ingredients for a chef salad.

The first three are benign. Clients who had called to say thank you or ask a question.

The fourth is anything but.

For several seconds there is only a rough and raspy breathing, followed by a growled three-word message that somehow manages to both anger me and chill me to my core.

Miss me yet?

I immediately check the call log, fighting back a shudder when I see it. All the numbers but one pop up on the display, and I can clearly see that each of those calls had been forwarded from my office across town to my cell phone.

The lone standout that reads 'unavailable' makes the hair on the back of my neck stand on end. My personal cell phone number is not publicly available. Only trusted friends have direct access to me that way. For my clients, routing calls through my office to my cell phone is my standard protocol. I have always tried to be very diligent about maintaining a buffer between personal and professional, even more so lately since a good friend and fellow realtor was assaulted in a vacant property a few years ago by an infatuated acquaintance.

So how the hell did someone get my number?

Although I really do not want to, I listen to the message again, eyes closed, straining to hear any familiarity in the deep, snarling tone.

Please God, not him. Please God, not him...

But try as I might, I cannot place the voice at all, and with relief I release the breath I did not even realize I'd been holding in.

"It's a wrong number, or a prank call," I mutter with conviction, and steeling my nerves, I delete the disturbing voicemail and return to preparing my salad.

That accomplished, I refill my wineglass, pick up my bowl of salad, and move to the couch to flip channels while I eat.

But in the back of my mind, I replay the mysterious caller's message repeatedly.

"Stop it," I chide myself. "That message wasn't meant for you. It was a misdial. Let it go."

By the time I place my empty bowl and wineglass in the dishwasher and head for bed, I have managed to convince myself that it was a fluke.

CHAPTER TWO
Allen

"Why are you still here?" I ask as I pause and lean against my best friend and business partner's open doorway.

"I could ask you the same thing," Grant replies with a grin. "What time is it, exactly?"

"Almost seven-thirty."

"Explains why I'm hungry," he quips. "I'm about to head out. What about you?"

"Another half-hour, tops," I reply.

"Careful," he says as he logs off his computer. "I'm beginning to think you ought to just move in here and save a rent payment."

"Partly your fault, you know," I shoot back with a grin. "This place has everything but a shower."

"Hey, I like happy employees. Happy employees are loyal employees – and productive," he reminds me.

"True. And we spend so much time here that it is just as well we have all the bells and whistles," I agree. "Or most of them, anyway. See you tomorrow."

I wander back down the hall to my office, Grant's chuckle still lingering in my ears.

But I was not kidding, I acknowledge. *We have made it a point to make this place an extremely attractive work environment, and it has paid off. We have one hell of a team here. Every single one of them is loyal and enthusiastic about the company's success.*

In fact, we have such a good team in place that I think it is time to tell Grant I am leaving.

I just hope he understands.

***

A half-hour later I am heading to the parking garage to return to the apartment I hate. For a while, I had no strong feelings one way or another; it had just been a place to crash for a few hours when I wasn't at work.

But with new neighbors to my left that yell and scream at each other constantly, and a family to my right with a brand-new and colicky baby, sleep has been next to impossible lately.

Really need to just buckle down and buy a house somewhere, I admit as I start my truck. *But since I am not sure I'm even going to stay in Austin, there's no point in looking yet.*

***

The drive home is uneventful, which is lucky, because Fight-Night Couple, as I have dubbed them, are *already* in full swing, which means unsolicited drama for anyone within earshot to endure. I can hear them the moment I pull into my designated parking space in front of my second-story apartment.

"Gonna be a long night," I mumble to myself as I walk up the stairs to my front door.

I let myself in, throw my keys on the kitchen counter, and grab a paper plate to dump my drive-through burger and fries out onto before moving to the sofa and picking up the remote control.

One round through the channels convinces me that throwing myself into a TV show with my headphones on is not a viable option. I sigh and move to my computer table instead. I slide my earbuds into place, then smile as the opening notes from Avenged Sevenfold's *Nightmare* album kick in to drown out Fight-Night Couple.

"That's more like it," I say, grinning, as I take a bite of my bacon cheeseburger, then open my email account and begin to type.

I work and hum along to the music for an hour, and when I stand and remove my earbuds, I am pleasantly surprised to realize that the noisy couple next door opted to call it a draw early.

"Things are looking up," I observe wryly as I throw my paper plate away then head to the bedroom. A quick shower precedes my pulling on pajama bottoms and crawling into my king-sized bed.

I have just about drifted off to sleep when the Johnson's newborn begins to wail, and I can't stop myself from laughing softly at the irony even as I grab the spare pillow and put it over my head to help muffle the noise.

No matter what else happens, I have got *to find another place to live.*

CHAPTER THREE
Brielle

After a deep sleep with no dreams that I can remember, I wake breathing heavily, exhausted to the bone, and covered in a thin but cloying layer of sweat. I immediately stretch my right hand out to tap the button on my alarm clock, silencing the aggressive, noisy peal that threatens to lead off my long day by conjuring a headache.

Why am I so tired? It's not like I was up late...

A glance down at my tangled sheets provides a clue.

Huh. Must not have slept as peacefully as I thought.

I throw back the twisted cotton, swing my legs over the side of the bed and sit up, rubbing my eyes as I yawn. I have never been that much of a morning person, and still find it hard to believe I chose a profession that many times calls for being not just awake, but *functional*, before ten a.m.

Chuckling to myself at the familiar battle in my brain - *Six o'clock. Seriously? Is the sun even up yet?* - I make myself stand up and stumble toward the bathroom for a quick shower.

"If people only knew what it costs me to set eight o'clock appointments," I grumble under my breath, then yawn again as I turn the handle and wait for the water to come up to an acceptable temperature.

The cool dampness of my skin reminds me I had been sweating when I woke. I frown at myself in my bathroom mirror as I quickly brush out the tangles in my shoulder-length brown hair.

They said I would probably hit menopause quickly after my hysterectomy, but that was years ago... lucky it took this long, I guess. I need to remember to ask Dr. Adranis if there is anything that can help with night sweats at my next appointment.

My frown deepens when the memories of why the surgery had even been necessary threaten to surface, and I tamp them down.

Hard.

Nope. Not today, I tell myself firmly, and make myself concentrate instead on getting rid of every tangle.

A faint ripple of movement in the mirror catches my attention, and I notice a small cloud of steam rising from the open top of the glass-walled shower behind me.

Finally. It's taking longer and longer for the water to get hot. Note to self - may be time for a new water heater. Sigh. Another addition to my 'fixer-upper-when-I-have-time' list...

Turning, I close the distance to the shower. I slide open the glass door, step in, and slide the door closed again, reveling in the warmth that immediately wraps around me like a blanket. Putting my back to the showerhead, I tilt my head back and wet my hair thoroughly before pumping shampoo from the dispenser into my hand and lathering it into my hair. The familiar fragrance of vanilla soothes my semi-sleepy awareness, dragging me softly and gradually toward fully awake.

By the time I rinse out the shampoo, replace it with equally fantastic-smelling leave-in conditioner, and reach for my loofah and body soap, my brain has snapped to attention and is racing down the list of the day's tasks.

Let's see... meet the Millers at eight at the Esters property for the first of four showings. Two conference calls - or was it three? I need to check that - followed by the open house on Prescott Avenue from noon to two today. Then two closings. Oh, and I need to follow up with Anne at some point today about the bidding war on that warehouse...

The frown I had worn earlier returns as I step out of the shower and towel off, then blow-dry my hair before I twist it upward into a sleek chignon.

The warehouse property has me puzzled. While its location is decent - at the edge of a well-established and high-traffic industrial complex - I personally do not think it's worth the extreme attention the site has garnered of late. What started off being a relatively easy set of circumstances veered into complication overnight. My client and at least one other party that I am aware of are fighting to claim that location as their own.

I might understand the competition over it if the existing building was in sound condition. But it isn't. Not by a long shot. 'Derelict' is even too kind a term. Frankly, even the cost to raze it to the ground and start over from scratch more than outweigh its current market value. Pile on a City Planning and Zoning Commission with a very narrow and inflexible scope of what the property can and cannot be used for, and the whole situation has become a nightmare. I have tried to persuade my client to focus a different direction, but he is intent on owning *that* warehouse.

Go down that rabbit hole later. For now, get dressed. Pick out comfortable shoes, too - you are going to do a lot of walking today.

Ugh.

I move to my closet and look once, longingly, at the left side where my jeans and t-shirts reside before I step dutifully to the right and grab a pale blue linen pantsuit that will at least allow for low-heeled shoes.

CHAPTER FOUR
Allen

We have been in our Wednesday morning meeting all of two minutes when I drop my bombshell on him. Grant stares open-mouthed at me from behind his desk before he finally finds his voice.

"What do you mean, you're *leaving*?"

"Just what I said," I reply calmly. "It's time. You knew going into this that I had plans to start up a security company. It's time for me to switch gears and focus on that."

"I know. I just didn't expect us to have this conversation before the first of *next* year."

"Grant, you've got a great thing here. It's solid, with an excellent team in place. Trust me, the way this company is structured, now is the optimal time for me to go my own direction. I'll still be your partner, Grant, just a silent one."

The younger man considers for a moment, then nods.

"Were you planning to stay around here?"

"I'm thinking a bit further north, actually. I have been considering the Dallas/Fort Worth area for a while now, specifically Pantego. It's situated about halfway between the two, so it's the ideal location."

"So, what comes next?"

"I'm going to travel up there next week and have a look around. Some friends of mine recommended a realtor that can help me find office space and a house."

Grant grins despite the circumstances.

"Not gonna do another apartment? Had your fill of yelling couples and screaming kids?"

I chuckle. "And how. Nope, I am going all in. A space all to myself that with any luck will have at *least* fifty feet of yard all the way around it so I can control how close my neighbors get."

"When do you think you'll make the move?"

"By the end of the summer, at the latest," I answer honestly. "At least, I hope it doesn't take longer than that. I have been restless for a while now. This is something I really want, Grant, and I need to get started."

Grant stands and extends his hand.

"Let me know if I can help in any way."

"Thanks, man."

***

When I get back to my desk, I pull out my cell phone and navigate to the last text message I had seen from Kenneth Myers, my roommate from college.

Here is the number of the realtor we used. Extremely helpful, knows her stuff. She will do right by you.

The text ends with a name and phone number.

Drumming my fingers on the desk, I dial and wait. Four rings later a rich, sultry tone fills my ear, making the blood in my veins rush to places that it has no business traveling to while I am sitting at my desk in an office with glass walls.

"You've reached the voicemail for Brielle Cerver," the smokey voice intones. "I'm terribly sorry to have missed your call. Please leave your name and number and I'll get back to you as soon as I can."

I clear my throat and fervently will my body's reaction away as I wait for the obligatory beep.

"Ms. Cerver, my name is Allen Jones," I say into the phone I am now gripping tightly in my effort to focus on the task at hand. "I'm looking to buy both residential and commercial property in Pantego, and you came highly recommended."

I pause, barely stopping myself from adding 'and you sound hot as hell'.

What are you, sixteen? Idiot. Get it together.

I clear my throat again and press on.

"If you could please call me back, I'd appreciate it. I'm planning to travel to that area next week and I'd like to line out some showings."

I finish the voicemail by reciting my number, then disconnect the call, and am immediately struck by the sudden urge to call her number a second time just to hear that sexy, breathtaking voice again.

Somehow, I overcome the impulse, and purposely wait several minutes to make sure I will not be embarrassed before I stand up to walk to the conference room for my ten o'clock planning session with the engineering group.

I nod at each team member as they enter the room and take their seats, pushing any thought of Brielle Cerver - and my very out-of-character reaction to her - firmly to the back of my mind for the moment.

CHAPTER FIVE
Brielle

One-thirty, I note as I tap my fingers idly on the kitchen counter. *Another half-hour of this. Man, I hope more people show up.*

To say I am disappointed is an understatement; I had hoped that the Prescott home would be overrun with prospective buyers during this span of unfettered access to the property.

There has been one so far.

Maybe the property's cursed, I think to myself, then giggle. I do not believe in such things. Nasty divorce proceedings, where the judge is making the couple sell and divide the proceeds? Now that, I *do* believe, because that is what is happening here.

Unfortunately, neither one of them listened to me when I advised them that the half-million-dollar listing price they insisted upon was much too high.

Now, four months later, this house has become my personal millstone. I have delivered in excess of fifteen fair and equitable offers for the property to my clients, but since they cannot agree to anything at all between them, we have reached a stalemate. Two more months of this and I will attain a new 'first' in my long career - reaching the end of the contractual period to act as the seller's agent and walking away.

Or in this case, running.

Wonder if I can get the judge to order them to pull their heads out and cooperate - and lower the price, I lament to myself as the last minutes of a fruitless open house drag out into infinity.

I am bored but obligated to stay put until the advertised end time, so I pull out my cell phone and begin listening to voicemails that accumulated throughout the morning. As I review them, I make notes in the peculiar shorthand I have developed over the years. Besides me, only my long-suffering assistant Rita can decipher it.

My hand pauses its movements with the pen when I listen to the eleventh voicemail.

A man's voice, deep and deliciously seductive. My skin forms goosepimples across my body as his sound washes over me, tightening my core with a sudden, almost painful stab of primal longing.

God, his voice is sex personified...

I am so entranced by it that I fail to capture one single piece of data from the voicemail.

I frown, shake my head, and pull the phone away from my ear long enough to press 'replay', determined to focus this time.

Allen Jones.

Residential and commercial property.

Next week.

By the time I reach the end of his voicemail again my knees are weak, and my pulse is pounding in my ears.

What the hell is the matter with you? That is a potential client. No-fly zone. Grow up!

Even though I am standing in a kitchen by myself, I take a moment to smooth my hair and breathe deeply, trying desperately to stifle both my embarrassment and a long-dormant need that Allen Jones' voice has caused to surface. After several minutes, I finally feel composed enough to attempt to return his call.

Just as I begin to dial, I hear, "Hello there! Are we too late to see the house?" from the front foyer. I tuck my phone back into my bag and move swiftly to greet the couple that have just arrived.

"Not at all," I say warmly, extending my hand to each of them in turn. "My name's Brielle. Let me show you around."

I lead, but only in the loosest sense of the word. I abhor hovering, pushy salespeople, and it carries over into my work. My preferred method of interaction is to quietly tell prospective buyers about certain amenities, then step out of the way and let their surroundings speak for themselves.

Obviously excited, the young woman turns to me with a smile and asks a question, which I readily answer. She nods her thanks, and they continue their self-guided tour while I retreat to the kitchen as I told them I would.

Just before two o'clock they approach me in the kitchen and ask about the deadline for submitting an offer. I hand them a fact sheet about the property and point out my office address and number before shaking their hands again and watching them leave.

Maybe this house was just waiting for them to arrive, I think to myself as I walk through the property and make sure all the lights are turned off before returning to the kitchen to collect my bag.

I step outside the front door, locking it securely behind me, then head to my car for the drive to the first of two closings I have this afternoon.

***

It is a little after five o'clock before I have a chance to return any phone calls. Although part of me wants to skip ahead to Allen Jones, it is only fair that I return them in the order received.

Luckily for me, only six of the first ten voicemails I received require a callback from me; the other four were purely informational, such as Miss Carmichael confirming the title company's receipt of the corrected documents.

I swing by my favorite Chinese takeout place for my usual chicken fried rice before heading home. Once I have eaten, I settle in at my computer, take a deep breath, grab my notepad, and dial the number that leads to that hypnotizing voice.

Given that it is now dinnertime for most families, I am expecting to have to leave a voicemail of my own. So much so that when a murmured, "Hello?" comes across the line to me, I almost drop my phone.

CHAPTER SIX
Allen

I mute the television, glance at the incoming number, and smile.

It's her, I think gleefully, then roll my eyes at my juvenile reaction.

Be cool, dude. Be cool...

I press the button to answer and murmur, "Hello?"

Silence at first, followed by, "I'm sorry to disturb you. I am returning a phone call from a Mr. Allen Jones. Might he be available?"

"Speaking. Mrs. Cerver?" I ask deliberately, hoping she will correct me on the assumed marital status.

She does not disappoint.

"Yes, this is Miss Cerver, but please, call me Brielle."

"Certainly, Brielle," I reply, "but only if you'll call me Allen."

She laughs, a light, throaty sound that inflames my senses and makes the arousal I experienced earlier today seem like amateur hour.

Thank God I am alone in my apartment.

"Sure, Allen," she says, and my name rolling off her tongue is pure music.

"So," she continues, "I know you mentioned you're looking for both a home to purchase and commercial property. What areas of North Texas did you have in mind specifically?"

It takes everything I have not to respond like a randy teenager and say, "I'm much more interested in *your* areas."

This woman's going to drive me crazy with just her voice.

"I was targeting Pantego, actually, since it's between Dallas and Fort Worth. Of course, you know that market much better than I do. I'd prefer to have both my house and business based there, but I would settle for living in Pantego and buying the commercial property within a half-hour's drive."

"Makes sense. Why drive further than thirty minutes to work if you don't have to?" Brielle teases, then pauses for a moment, and I close my eyes and just listen to her breathe and type on her keyboard.

She asks a few more questions to narrow down the type of home I am looking for, and the soft gasp I hear when it becomes clear to her that I am single intrigues me.

It intrigues me a great deal.

"So, when can I come meet you and tour some properties?"

"You can come see me anytime," she answers immediately, then gasps again, and says, "Oh, my... that didn't come out right... I'm so sorry... what I meant was, you can come look at the *properties* anytime you'd like..."

Her sweet, sexy, smokey voice trails off in an embarrassment that I can feel through the phone, and I find it strangely endearing.

"It's all right, Brielle," I say, trying and failing to keep the laughter out of my tone. "I knew what you meant. How about this weekend?"

"Hold on a moment, let me pull up my planner," she manages, and I can hear the humor building in her voice, too.

"Yes," she confirms to me. "I'm a little shocked to see it, actually, but this Saturday and Sunday are both wide open at the moment. All the commercial spots and most of the homes I think you would be interested in are unoccupied, so we will be able to access them and look around, not a problem at all. Where would you like to meet?"

"Your office?"

"Sure. What is your email? I'll send you my contact information and directions."

We talk a few minutes longer, and with each word I find myself more and more drawn to this mystery woman with a voice like crushed velvet.

Finally, the conversation stalls into an awkward silence before she says, "So... Saturday. Around nine? And a couple of the commercial sites are a bit rough. I recommend jeans - or at least *not* anything that needs to be dry cleaned."

I realize I am completely hopeless when her words immediately summon a vision of a shapely backside clad in form-fitting denim.

We end the call shortly afterward, and my curiosity gets the best of me. I immediately navigate to her website to check out the face that belongs with that amazing voice.

And my heart triple-thumps when I see her.

The look is similar enough that Brielle could easily be mistaken for Mary's sister. If she had blond hair and blue eyes instead of dark brown and emerald eyes, they might even have passed for twins.

My Mary.

My hand falters on the mouse as bittersweet memories surge forward and threaten to wreck me completely.

It was two days after her third round of chemo was completed. When the doctors told us that the inoperable tumor robbing her of not just her sight but her life had gotten bigger, not smaller, and that the cancer had spread, Mary's patience finally ran out.

"Enough," she had said abruptly. "No more. I am done. Allen, take me home."

She was quiet for most of the forty-five-minute ride back to our house in the suburbs, her scarf-wrapped head tilted back gently against the padded headrest, her eyes closed, her hand out the window making fluttering motions in the late spring breeze as we drove.

We had just pulled into our driveway when she opened her baby blue eyes and looked my direction.

"Allen," she said, her voice almost at a whisper.

"Yes?"

"When I am gone, you need to move on, honey. Do not shut yourself off from the world. Find love again."

I started to protest but she stopped me with one frail finger to my lips.

"Baby," Mary said in earnest, "promise me. Please."

"I promise," I replied, my voice almost hoarse with the lie.

My Mary left me for good eighteen days later and took my heart right along with her. That was almost ten years ago.

And up until now, I have found it impossible to keep that promise. Up until hearing Brielle Cerver speak, I was perfectly content to merely drift along, focused on nothing but making it through another day.

I somehow manage to make my way to my bedroom, with no recollection whatsoever of leaving my couch. I strip off my clothes, lie down on my huge and painfully empty king-sized bed, and stare at the ceiling for what seems like hours.

When I do manage to finally fall asleep, I hear Mary's voice in my mind, telling me in her soft, warm tones that I need to remember my promise to her - that I would not spend the rest of my life alone.

CHAPTER SEVEN
Brielle

I stare at the phone in my hand, my mind a complete blank, trying my best to process everything I am feeling.

Hearing him speak to me on the voicemail he left me was arousing enough. But hearing that deep Texas drawl in real time, complete with the sexy-as-hell chuckle woven through that magic tone?

Orgasm-inducing. Just this side of it, anyway.

I seriously need a drink.

With effort, I stand on suddenly wobbly legs and head for the fridge and the Moscato. I pour a half-glass, pause, consider, then top it off before I put the bottle back where it goes.

I am not sure what is happening here, but I cannot do this, I tell myself after the first sip. *So much is wrong with this scenario. Getting involved with a client, for one. Not to mention it has been forever since I've...*

That thought alone prompts a second, much larger drink as my freak-out begins in earnest.

So how to extricate myself from this situation? We have already set a day and time to meet.

And? my logical side counters. *Put your hormones back in the box, sister. He has a nice voice, that's all. Nothing more than that. Chill out and do your job Saturday. Besides, this... this... whatever-this-is is most likely one-sided. So, play it cool. He is just another client that needs your help. End of story.*

"Right," I mutter aloud after another long swallow, then grimace as I realize I am standing alone in my gourmet kitchen arguing with myself.

"Maybe I *should* get a pet," I grumble. "At least then I'd have another living creature to talk to instead of myself like a crazy person."

The abrupt ring of my cell phone startles me enough that I spill a bit of wine over the rim of my glass. I pivot to grab first my phone, then a paper towel to mop up the small splash on my floor.

"Hey Mari, what's up?" I say, as I straighten up again and throw the paper towel away.

I first met Maribella - or 'Mari', as she prefers to be called - in a spin class ten years ago. While my New Year's resolution that year only lasted about five weeks, the best friend I gained was well worth it.

"I sensed a disturbance in the force," she teases now. "Something just told me to call and check on you. Have you eaten yet?"

"Grabbed Chinese earlier."

"Good," Mari says firmly. "Then I'm not out of line bringing dessert with me. Cheesecake. I'll be there in ten."

She's gone before I have the chance to protest.

She is smart, I'll give her that. She knows cheesecake is my weakness, I acknowledge with a smile.

***

Mari is punctual, as always, and at minute twelve we have two slices of cheesecake plated and are settling in at my kitchen table.

"Spill it," she commands, pointing at me with her fork before she scoops up her first bite.

I shrug my shoulders with a huge sigh and wade right in, telling her all about both interactions with Allen Jones and my strong and unexpected reaction to each one.

"Wow," she says thoughtfully, pausing to delicately pat the corner of her mouth with a napkin.

There is a lot of power in that one-word response of hers, and she and I both know it. She is the only one in my new life that I ever confided in about what happened to me; the only one that knows the story. She is also the only one besides me who knows that my journey from Becka Corgan, shattered survivor, to Brielle Cerver, self-sufficient, confident businesswoman, was fraught with nightmares for years.

"Honey," she says gently, laying her hand over mine, "even if it *does* turn out to be one-sided, it's still a blessing, Bri. Means you are healing, finally. Enough to feel something again."

"What should I do?" I blurt out, feeling completely out of control.

"Take things as they come - and trust your gut, Brielle. That's all you can do."

CHAPTER EIGHT
Allen

I spend the two days leading up to meeting Brielle Cerver consumed with a dark, brooding self-loathing that not even Grant's sincere "You know I'm here for you, right?" can overcome.

Seeing the realtor's picture Wednesday night reopened an abyss of heartache for me, and it felt like Mary's death happened only yesterday. And that was immediately followed by guilt - earned or not - because I have never gotten over losing Mary, and part of me feels like even *thinking* about another woman is a severe betrayal.

I hate myself for every thought I have had so far about Brielle Cerver, no matter what the Mary in my dreams tries to tell me, and I am determined as hell to keep the woman with the smokey voice at arm's length.

In fact, I consider calling her back on Friday evening to cancel the meeting altogether before I realize that doing so is not fair to Brielle.

Not her fault I have issues, I tell myself grimly. *Meet her, tour the properties, buy if they are right for what I want, move on. Purely business. Nothing more than that.*

After a third restless night, I am up at three-twenty a.m. on Saturday morning. I shower and dress in jeans, boots, and a polo shirt before I make myself some scrambled eggs, toast, and coffee.

There is no good reason to be up before four a.m. Even with traffic, the drive from Austin to Pantego is typically less than four hours. And before six a.m. on a weekend, traffic is nonexistent.

But I am itching to get today's events done and over with.

I pour a second cup of coffee into my travel mug, then lock my front door. I am programming Brielle Cerver's office address into the GPS in my truck, then backing out of my parking space, at four-fifteen.

With each mile marker I pass on north I-35, my gut clenches just a bit more. Annoyed with myself, I turn on my radio, hoping to get lost in the mechanics of the drive and the flow of the music and not feel anything.

It is so much better when I don't feel anything, I tell myself.

By the time I pull into the parking lot in front of the small but tidy one-story brick building that serves as Brielle Cerver's office, I have almost convinced myself that's true.

Taking a deep breath to steel my nerves, I park my truck, then exit, walking slowly toward the front door. A small sign displayed in neat script reveals Brielle's office hours, and I note that weekends are by appointment only.

Although I am ten minutes early, the door opens easily when I tug gently on its wrought-iron handle. I step inside and notice a woman seated at the reception desk ahead.

"Mr. Jones?"

"Yes, ma'am, that's me."

"Good morning. Miss Cerver's on her way, she should be here any time now. Can I interest you in some coffee?"

"No thanks, I've had some."

"Very well, let me know if you need anything. I'm Rita."

I glance around, then walk toward the overstuffed armchair that affords a view out of the front window. I settle into the comfortable seat, wondering if the intense bout of nerves that just hit me are evident. I risk looking back toward Rita's desk, but she is typing away merrily on her keyboard.

I barely contain a sigh of discomfort as I wait and bolster my determination to remain aloof all day.

I can do this, I tell myself. *I can keep it strictly professional.*

The sound of a car door closing catches my attention, and I look to my right and out the window and watch Brielle Cerver walking toward the building.

Brielle's richly dark brown hair reveals gorgeous deep auburn highlights in the morning sun. Between that, the form-fitting jeans she is wearing, and the sway of her hips as she moves, I can already tell that today will be a much bigger challenge than I thought.

CHAPTER NINE
Brielle

He is not just punctual, he's early, I note when I pull into the parking lot of my office at eight-fifty-two and see an unfamiliar truck already occupying a space. *Good to know we have that in common.*

I step out of my car, wincing at the humidity that already seems a bit oppressive for so early on a mid-April morning. I look in my purse, noting with satisfaction that I remembered to pick up a ponytail band and my small brush.

That is the first order of business today, get all this hair pulled up out of my way, I tell myself as I lock my car and walk toward the door.

As I move up the sidewalk, I get the sensation of being watched, but since I opted to have the front windows of my office tinted, I cannot confirm my suspicion. It is not until I walk through the door that I know my hunch is right.

"Morning, Rita," I say as I enter, but my attention is immediately drawn to my left, where the most gorgeous man I have ever laid eyes on is occupying the leather armchair and staring back at me.

Well, hello there, tall dark and handsome...

I feel certain that my smile is over bright, and I'm struggling to project professionalism when I say, "Good morning, nice to meet you in person, finally. Just let me grab a few things and we'll get started."

He responds only with a cool nod, his face devoid of expression, and a wave of confusion courses through me.

Huh. Maybe he isn't a morning person either?

I reluctantly swing my gaze toward Rita, who has cleared her throat to get my attention and is holding out a small stack of messages.

"From the voicemail," she says, thrusting them my direction.

"Thanks," I reply. "I'll just be a moment."

With another glance toward my new client, I step around the reception desk and walk down the narrow hallway behind Rita, trying my best to project an easy confidence as I leave Allen's presence.

Once I reach my destination and quietly close the door, I let my breath out again.

That man is stunning, I admit to myself in the mirror over the half-bath sink as I quickly brush my hair up and into a ponytail. *More than I even thought possible. Black hair, goatee, blue-grey eyes, strong jaw, and I bet those muscles are not confined to his arms. I wonder if he's got washboard abs...*

That line of thought makes my cheeks tinge pink, and I purposefully shut it down.

Client. Property. Focus.

I take several deep breaths to center myself, then check my appearance one last time in the mirror before I get moving again.

A sharp right turn leads to my office, where I place the messages on my desk and pick up the folder with today's showing list, before I head back to the reception area to begin my day with a man that I swear could easily grace the cover of any magazine.

As I step back into the front lobby, Allen's gaze sweeps over me, from my head to my shoes and back again. The glimmer of heat that shines in his eyes is a mere flash - I blink, and it's gone again, his face schooled into a neutral expression.

What was that?

Trying my best to not make my sudden and intense attraction to him obvious, I gently clear my throat.

"Ready to go?" I ask breezily.

The one-word, sexily growled answer from him stirs my arousal from embers to full-on flames.

"Yes," Allen says, piercing me with a gaze full of lustful promise before his emotionless mask slips back into place.

CHAPTER TEN
Allen

God help me, she smells like vanilla. I pick up the scent the moment she walks in the front door of her office, and it makes me so hard that I'm glad I'm sitting down so I can hide my reaction to her.

Brielle speaks, but I honestly do not hear a damn thing she says because I am so focused on her full lips and wondering what they might feel like, taste like, pressed against mine.

When she stops and looks at me expectantly I merely nod, hoping like hell that the raging lust I am feeling for her is not advertised all over my face.

She falters, and I can see a thin ribbon of confusion stream across her face before she turns her attention to her receptionist, who has been watching Brielle with a slightly amused expression.

Brielle excuses herself and disappears down the hall, and I return my focus to looking out the window and thinking about math equations, and basketball, and anything else that will make my erection disappear before I have to stand and walk with her.

Mary.

That not only douses the flames, but it turns the guilt-o-meter up a thousand percent.

Mary would want you to move on, part of my brain reminds me, and I hold in a snarl of contempt.

Approaching footsteps garner my attention, and I swivel my head just in time to see Brielle come into view again. I cannot help myself. Despite my best efforts, I cannot help but stare, long and hard, up and down her delectable little body.

Keep your shit together, my psyche prods, and the lust is shoved roughly aside.

"Ready to go?" Brielle asks, and my self-control is severely tested at her unintended innuendo.

Like you would not believe, I almost blurt out, but catch myself.

"Yes," I manage, my voice a growl with the effort it takes to rein myself in.

I stand, reciting the Pythagorean theorem in my head, and follow her outside, purposely looking anywhere but at that firm butt of hers showcased so nicely by her jeans.

"I thought we'd ride together if that's all right. We can take my car," Brielle offers.

No, no, no, that is a horrible idea. Proximity is a recipe for disaster.

"No," I bark, a little sharper than I intended, and notice her flinch at my tone.

Smooth, dude, real smooth. You make it sound like she has the plague or something.

Frustrated with myself, I try to explain to erase the surprise - and hurt that she is unable to hide quickly enough - flitting across her features.

"I think separate cars is a good idea. That way when we're done you don't have to drive me back."

"Oh," she says, and looks a little disappointed before she shrugs her shoulders. "Makes sense, I guess. Very well, then. Follow me."

She pivots and moves to her vehicle as I continue toward mine, berating myself with every step.

It's going to be a very long day.

CHAPTER ELEVEN
Brielle

It is almost six o'clock before I make it back to my house, and my head is reeling from the day's very strange turn of events. The day had, as I expected, been awkward - but not in the way I envisioned.

Other than a couple of searing glances thrown my way in my front lobby, there was no spark between Allen and me all day long.

Not one.

As a matter of fact, it sure seemed like he didn't want to be anywhere near me. He couldn't get away from me fast enough, I realize as I move to my kitchen where my stalwart hero, Moscato, beckons to me.

"I just don't get it," I mutter as I pour. "Could've sworn the other night on the phone that there was a connection."

Man, had I been completely - hopelessly - misguided in that notion.

Well, at least I know for sure now that it was one-sided, I admit to myself with a sad sigh. *Sexy voice and good looking, but kind of a jackass. Go figure.*

The saving grace of the day had been that Allen - *Mr. Jones,* I auto-correct in my head - found both a residence and a commercial property here in Pantego that he wishes to buy. Our afternoon together had wrapped with him brusquely telling me to move forward with offers on each.

Closing my eyes, I recount the last moments before he got back in his truck and drove away from me...

I extend my hand, and he hesitates, then slowly wraps his strong fingers around mine.

The instant we touch I feel something spring to life between us, a massive surge of connection that raises gooseflesh on me from head to toe. I suppress a gasp, my eyes widening in surprise, and glance up at his face to see if he feels it as well. And I see the briefest glimpse of... something... causing his blue-grey eyes to darken as they look back into mine.

Then he abruptly drops my hand, takes one step back, and the moment is gone, vanished into thin air like it had never happened.

"Let me know when I need to sign closing papers," he states solemnly, his eyes blank, the look on his face indecipherable.

I nod silently, still trying to process everything I am feeling in that moment as he turns on his heel, gets into his truck, and drives away like his very life depends on putting as much distance as possible between us...

"Well, no worries about treating him as just another client, I suppose," I acknowledge now, attempting to cheer myself up as I refill my glass.

After all, that's what I wanted, was to keep things professional. Right?

Right.

Wineglass in hand, I move to my bathroom and begin to fill my garden tub. I take down my ponytail and am brushing out my hair when a small voice in my head pipes up with a random - and unwanted - observation.

Okay, then. So why does his rejection sting so much?

As I undress and sink into the steamy water, I am dismayed to realize I have no good answer to that question.

***

Forty minutes later I get a call from Mari.

"So," she begins in a sing-song voice, "how did today go? Is he handsome?"

"Like you wouldn't believe. Too bad he's also a jackass," I tell her honestly.

"What? Why? What happened?"

I sigh, then fill her in on how my day went.

"Oh. That sucks," she commiserates, and although she can't see me, I nod along in agreement.

"Yep," I exhale heavily. "It is what it is."

"But hey, look on the bright side. You now know you are capable of being attracted to someone again. It's a good thing, Bri."

That's my Mari, always 'sunny side up' for me.

What she doesn't realize is that I have zero intention of unleashing my newly returned 'ability'. I am much better off alone, especially if all it nets me is disappointment like it did today.

I will help Mr. Jones acquire his new home and commercial space like I said I would, and then I am done.

Good riddance, I think to myself, knowing somewhere deep down that only part of me means it.

CHAPTER TWELVE
Allen

I am a complete idiot. There are no two ways about it. And an asshole, to boot.

I only meant to keep Brielle at arm's length, that's it. Just to keep from succumbing to temptation. Instead, I swung too far the other direction and was a complete jerk to her all day.

I was so effective, in fact, that even if I *did* decide to pursue something with her, I think I have officially blown any chance I might have had.

I am still amazed that Brielle didn't just toss me the list of properties and walk away at one point. She could have. By all rights, she *should* have.

But she didn't. She kept her cool despite my clipped, icy tone and generally rude behavior.

I bang the steering wheel in frustration.

Because at the very end of the exceptionally long, tense day I put her through, she stuck out her hand to say farewell. And when I touched her, I felt the universe shift all around us, through us, like some long-missing puzzle piece finally clicked into place. The want - the *need* - sparked between us like St. Elmo's fire.

I can still hear her drawing her breath in sharply, her intense gaze drifting its focus upward to meet mine. I can still see the fire of raw longing swirling in those emerald-green depths.

It took everything I had to step back, not forward to take her into my arms and kiss her like she's never been kissed before.

And to top it off, I barked orders at her then ran away as fast as I could.

It's a drive filled with shame all the way back to Austin.

I did the right thing, I stubbornly insist to myself as I crawl into bed, choosing to ignore the growing sense of loss that took root the moment I left Brielle standing by her car in downtown Pantego.

A ping from my laptop has me up and out of the bed that I am failing to fall asleep in. When I open my emails and see a new one from Brielle, my heart picks up its pace all on its own.

But as I read the message that she sent me it is crystal clear I did too much damage; I have never seen a more cold, impersonal narrative. A stiff, formal salutation followed by the offers I asked her to put together and ending with instructions detailing the next steps in the process.

All business, even her signature - *B. Cerver.*

As I deserve.

But that was what you wanted, right?

So why are you unhappy?

I ponder that question the rest of the night, and the breaking dawn finds me still searching for the answer.

CHAPTER THIRTEEN
Brielle

"Good morning, Rita. Lots to do today," I announce as I arrive at my office building bright and early four Mondays later. "Two closings, among other things."

"We actually have *four* closings, not two. The Jones closings are this afternoon," she reminds me. "Don't you plan on going?"

I shrug my shoulders.

"I really don't see the need," I tell her, my stiff posture at odds with the nonchalant way I attempt my answer. "He's paying cash, the title company overnighted him the documents for both properties, and the sellers' realtors are leaving the keys in each lockbox for him. No, there's nothing more I need to do for Mr. Jones."

Never have to interact with him ever again, actually. What a relief, I think to myself.

"Ah. I've already started the coffee for you," she chimes back, transitioning smoothly away from that prickly topic with a knowing smile.

"You're a lifesaver. Don't know what I'd do without you."

"You could lock up tonight. I need to leave at four. I've got a date."

"Deal."

As I walk back to our tiny kitchen to pour myself a cup, I mentally shake off the simultaneous irritation and interest that happens every time I even *think* of Allen Jones. Which, sadly, is more often than I would like to admit.

Enough. Focus, I chide myself as I add creamer and sugar and stir rapidly, then sip to confirm that it is ready to enjoy.

I sit behind my desk, boot up my computer, and turn my attention to the lovely young couple whose closing later this morning means that my personal millstone is about to be a successful sale instead of a black mark on my track record. I had been right about my gut feeling - the Prescott home, trapped for so long between warring soon-to-be-ex-spouses, is finally about to become the residence for a new family.

Looking back, that sparsely attended two-hour open house turned out to be a blessing, I think to myself with a smile. *Everything happens for a reason.*

***

I sail through my busy schedule - the two closings sandwiched between three showings and another open house - with no major issues. I lock up my office and arrive home a little after six p.m.

I have just settled in to making myself some pasta for dinner when my cell phone rings. When I glance at the screen, the blood in my body runs cold.

Unavailable, the display reads.

I freeze, holding my breath, as the phone rings four times, then goes silent.

A few moments later, a sharp ping lets me know I have a new voicemail message.

With a shaking hand, I reach out and tap the icon to play the message.

"Good evening, Bri... Miss Cerver," I hear Allen's rich baritone say. "I was just calling to say thank you for all your hard work. Both closings happened today, and they went off without a hitch."

His message to me pauses, then continues, "But I'm sure you already knew that. Anyway..."

Wait. What is that I'm hearing in his voice? Regret?

"Maybe once I get settled in up there, we can meet for dinner. It is the least I can do to thank you for all your help. Okay, then. Guess I will talk to you later. Have a good night."

I stare at the phone for a long moment, completely conflicted as to what I should do. Then I remember the way he acted the one and only day we spent time together, and my resolve hardens.

I press 'delete' and send his voicemail into tech oblivion before I turn my attention back to the boiling water on my stove.

Ten minutes later, my phone rings again. When I see the 'unavailable' designation come up once more, I lift an eyebrow.

"What more can he possibly have to say?" I mutter under my breath, and purposely ignore the new voicemail notification.

It is not until my pasta is plated that I decide to listen to whatever new awkward message Allen Jones has left me. I pick up my phone with my left hand and press 'play', then pick up my plate with my right hand, and move toward the table.

My plate of fettucine hits my kitchen floor and shatters when I hear rasping, deep, ominous breathing, followed by four maliciously snarled words that leave me shivering.

"Your time's coming, bitch."

CHAPTER FOURTEEN
Allen

He's endured my crappy attitude for weeks now, and Grant has had enough.

"What's your problem lately? You've been impossible to deal with," he snaps at me the Monday morning I'm closing on the properties Brielle found for me.

I grumble under my breath before I finally confess it all - my unexpected reaction to her, the guilt, and my horrible treatment of Brielle the day we met in person.

It is Grant's suggestion that I call and try to make amends after I finally tell him why I am wound up so tightly that I've almost ceased to function like a normal person.

"You're only hurting yourself," he says gently. "Mary knew what she was doing when she made you make that promise. The way to honor her is to keep it."

I sigh and slump my shoulders.

"After the way I treated Brielle, I've blown it. I just know it."

"Maybe you did blow it," he acknowledges. "But maybe not. You won't know for sure unless you try."

That evening I gather up my courage and call her. When it goes to her voicemail, I extend my olive branch, and settle down to wait it out.

Three days pass with no response from Brielle, so I try her office number during daytime hours and connect with Rita, who promptly takes my name and number and assures me she will pass along my request for Brielle to call me back.

After three more days pass and I still have not heard from her, I know for sure my earlier suspicion is correct.

I screwed up. Badly.

I tell Grant as much the following Monday morning, and he claps a sympathetic hand on my shoulder.

"I'm sorry, Allen," he says sincerely.

"Me too," I reply, and realize how much I mean it.

***

I spend the rest of my last week at Grant's company lining out the transition; my duties are being spread out among my two assistants. As planned, I will still be Grant's business partner, stepping back only from my current day-to-day role in the scheme of things.

By the time the moving van and crew arrives on Saturday morning, I am completely packed and ready to leave my current world behind for the future I am building in a little town four hours to the north.

And I might have had getting to know Brielle better to look forward to, if I had not been such an ass, I admonish myself, and shake my head.

I pull out of the apartment parking lot for the last time. The movers fall into line right behind me as we begin the drive toward my new start.

CHAPTER FIFTEEN
Brielle

"There's nothing you can do?" I ask the patient and polite detective who's arrived at my home on what should be a bright and cheery Saturday morning.

After a third creepy call, I have finally decided to get the authorities involved, but to my dismay, I'm learning quickly that their hands are pretty much tied.

"I'm sorry, but no, not really, not with what little we have," he replied. "That unavailable number isn't traceable, and without any sort of physical evidence, there's no way to try to figure out who's behind this."

"So, what do I do?"

"Keep a record of any more calls or messages you get. I will open a file on this and add notes about any other instances should anything else happen. But my strongest recommendations now are to change your phone number and maintain awareness of your surroundings. If things escalate, call us."

"Escalate?" I can feel my eyes widening in concern.

"If the calls and messages become more frequent or more intense, for example," he explains.

"Or if I feel like someone's following me," I say slowly, my mind racing with all sorts of unfathomable possibilities.

Yeah, just like... No. Do not go there!

The detective touches his hand to my arm.

"Are you all right, Miss Cerver? You're very pale."

"Sorry," I manage in a hoarse whisper. "It's just... I just... um. Had a really bad experience with an ex-boyfriend several years ago."

He leans forward and frowns, his eyebrows knitting together with worry.

"Is that so. Can you please tell me what happened?"

I explain an abbreviated version only, because even the highlight reel I am sharing threatens to undo the carefully constructed composure that I am barely managing to cling to thus far.

The seasoned detective takes notes as I talk, and I can tell by his expression that he has seen firsthand precisely the type of details I have just glossed over. When I am finished, he clears his throat gently, and I see both anger and sympathy reflected in his eyes when he speaks.

"I'm so sorry you went through that. If it will help put you at ease, I am happy to check into him and make sure he is still incarcerated. I will also make sure your new name does not come up anywhere at all in connection with all that. Okay?"

I heave a sigh of relief.

"Yes, please. That would be good," I say, and attempt a weak smile.

He leaves me with a reassuring smile, a card with the nearest station's address and direct dial number, and a report number, and my hands tremble as I close and lock my front door behind him.

That afternoon Mari and I head out shopping, and among my purchases is a can of mace and a brand-new phone with a brand-new number.

***

For the next few weeks, it is peaceful. My life returns to its normal level of hectic, with no further intimidating calls received. I begin to breathe easier, particularly when Detective Tucker stops by a few days after his first visit to let me know that my ex is still very much behind bars where he belongs.

But by the following Thursday my world begins to unravel again. Two more menacing voicemails followed by five text messages make it clear that whoever is fixated on me figured out my new number.

I immediately call the police so that Detective Tucker can add them to the open file.

Then I call Mari.

"I don't know what to do, Mari," I tell her despondently.

"Do you want to come and stay with me? Say the word. You know I have an extremely comfortable bed in the guest room."

"I know you do," I admit. "And I will keep that in mind. But I don't want you to be at risk, either. I will stay in my own place for now. Let's just hope that whoever has a problem with me doesn't feel the need to do anything more drastic than leave me hateful messages."

CHAPTER SIXTEEN
Allen

Six weeks post-move, I am sitting behind my desk, wrapping up the last interview with a new hire on Thursday afternoon.

Sam Jaxton's military service record is impressive, as is his prior experience providing personal security in the civilian sector. He is quiet, but when he does speak, it's well thought out and articulate.

The fact that he is a strapping six-foot-seven wall of muscle that has been trained to be lethal when necessary is a bonus.

Found my final member, I realize, and am grateful.

"Welcome to the team, Sam," I say, standing and extending my hand in congratulations.

"Thanks, Mr. Jones. I'm glad to be a part of this."

"Please, call me Allen. Glad to have you. Go down the hall and see Hope to get your onboarding paperwork completed. We will hit the ground running in the morning. Eight a.m. in the conference room."

"Yes, sir."

Once he's gone, I lean back in my chair and smile.

Sam's addition to my team means I now have six highly trained men in place to provide the best protection possible to those who come to us in need. Mark Baxter, retired Special Forces and unit leader, is the oldest at forty-three. Sam is forty, as is Braeden Nichols. The other three - Jack Anders, Marlon Gabriel, and Pete Dixon - are in their mid to late thirties.

While all of them have stellar military service backgrounds, Pete also brings guru-level IT skills to the group, which means that I have someone besides me that can discreetly access any system anywhere at any time.

Helping me keep track of it all - employees, clients, and the financial stuff that comes with running a business - is Hope Klosen, an experienced, no-nonsense accountant and office manager that I have known for years and trust completely.

Got a good group of people, I think to myself. *Should not take long for them to form a cohesive unit.*

I turn my attention to my computer and pull up my calendar for the next week. The client list is growing already, and I feel confident that with the contacts I have made with local law enforcement agencies, other people needing help will come my way sooner rather than later.

After all, there is only so much the police can do sometimes, I acknowledge, and repeat my company's simple but powerful mission statement in my head.

Protect and defend.

CHAPTER SEVENTEEN
Brielle

By lunchtime Friday, I sense that I am being watched everywhere I go, although I never see anyone or anything unusual. Still, the feeling makes me extremely uneasy.

For the first time in my career, I decide to have another realtor present with me during the open house I am hosting from two to four this afternoon. Anne is a competitor, but also a good friend, and when I explain the reason for my request, she readily agrees to keep me company.

"Don't forget, when Barbara got attacked, I was only two streets away at a showing," she reminds me. "That's when Benji made me promise I'd either learn to shoot or learn self-defense, since it's not always possible to buddy up for safety."

"Which did you choose?" I ask.

"Both," she says solemnly. "Can't be too careful."

The open house is well-attended, which enables me to focus on the event instead of my mysterious harasser. Too soon, I am shaking the hands of the last of the interested parties before Anne and I walk through the property together to turn off lights and close doors.

"Do you want me to follow you back to your office? I don't mind," she says, looking at me with concern like the protective fifty-nine-year-old grandmother of four that she is.

I wave her off, trying my best to sound braver than I feel.

"So far, it has just been voicemails and texts, nothing physical. I should be fine," I assure her.

We shake hands and part ways at the end of the driveway, but I notice that she lingers until I am in my car with my doors locked before she waves goodbye and drives off.

I call Mari, and her voice filling my car's speakers is a comfort.

"How did the open house go?" she asks.

"Pretty well," I tell her. "My gut says the Smiths will receive a few offers come Monday, if not by tonight."

"Good, I'm glad. Wanna go get sushi?"

"Sure. I missed lunch, and I am starved. You want to meet there, or should I come by and pick you up?"

"No point in both of us driving. You fly, I'll buy?"

"Deal," I answer with a grin. "I'll be there in a few minutes."

***

A half-hour later sees us settling into our usual booth at the hibachi and sushi place that has become a favorite haunt of ours. Our food arrives and we dig in. I am telling her about the open house when my phone chirps.

When I glance down and see 'unavailable', the color leaves my face. Mari notices it immediately.

"Another one?" she says softly, and I nod.

She holds out her hand. "Gimme."

I pass my phone to her and watch as she clicks on the text message icon to open the app. Her eyebrows raise as she reads the newest arrival, then glances up at me.

My words almost tangle in my suddenly constricted throat.

"What does it say?" I manage to whisper.

"You're definitely going to want to tell Detective Tucker about this one," Mari answers, and her face radiates concern as she turns the screen to where I can see it clearly.

Uppity bitch. You're gonna bleed.

The words are bad enough, but it is the picture underneath that sends my pulse into orbit. It is me, earlier today, as Anne and I unlocked the front door of the property to set up for the open house.

"Do... do you think..." I begin to stammer, but Mari cuts me off.

"I think that Anne being with you is the only thing that kept you safe today," she snaps, "and I think we need to call Tucker, right now."

Luckily, he is on duty, and dispatch puts me through to him in his car.

"I'm on my way to you," he says. "I'm not far from that restaurant. See you in a bit."

Detective Tucker arrives in minutes, and his jaw sets like granite when he sees the latest message sent to me.

"Ms. Cerver, I think it's time to consider hiring some personal security," he tells me, his voice firm.

He scrolls through his cell phone, then jots down something on one of his cards and hands it to me.

Cosantóirí LLC is followed by a phone number.

"You need to call them," he says earnestly. "A friend of mine works there, and they're really good at what they do. When you call, tell them Marlon's friend Adam Tucker sent you. Okay?"

I nod slowly. "Do you think it's safe for me to go home?"

"I think it's a good idea for me to at least follow you and check your house before you go inside if you insist on going home," he answers.

I nod again, my mind racing, as I dial the number I have been given, and wait.

"Cosantóirí LLC," I hear a woman's voice say.

"Hello, I was referred to you by Adam Tucker, he's a friend of Marlon's?"

The woman asks a few questions, then tells me, "I can send someone to meet you at your home within the next hour, if you'd like."

"Yes, please," I answer gratefully, and give her my name and address. When I hang up the call, I already feel a bit lighter.

"They'll meet us at my house around six," I announce to Mari and Detective Tucker, who both look relieved.

CHAPTER EIGHTEEN
Allen

I am just about to wrap up for the day when Hope appears in my doorway.

"Brand new client," she begins as she hands me an intake sheet. "And she sounded scared. I told her I would have someone at her place by six. Who do you want to send?"

As I skim the paper Hope just gave me, I do a doubletake, and Hope notices my reaction.

"You know her."

Yeah, I know her. She is the awesome woman I am severely attracted to that I treated like crap and drove away...

"She was my realtor," I answer instead, trying my best to sound calm and level. "She helped me find this place."

Brielle's one of the most strong, confident women I have ever met. If she is scared, it must be serious.

"What did she say when she called, exactly?"

"That a friend of Marlon's recommended us. An Adam Tucker."

"He's a detective with Pantego PD," I reveal, a note of worry tinging my tone that has Hope arching an eyebrow at me.

Whatever is going on is bad enough that the police referred her to us to keep her safe?

"So, who do you want to send?" Hope repeats.

I answer immediately.

"I'll take the lead on this one personally."

"And who do you want as your backup?" she tosses back, reminding me of one of my own basic rules - no one goes into a situation without backup.

"Marlon. But put him on standby only for now, please."

"You got it."

As Hope heads down the hall to read Marlon in, I turn off my laptop and pack it into its bag, then shrug on my suit jacket.

Ten minutes later I am in my truck, programming my GPS to take me right to Brielle Cerver's front door. As I leave the parallel space in front of my building, I can only hope that she will even speak to me once I arrive.

CHAPTER NINETEEN
Brielle

Mari insists on paying for our late lunch as agreed before we lead Detective Tucker back to my place. When we arrive, he holds out his hand for my keys.

"Alarm code?" he asks.

I flush scarlet.

"Well... um... about that..." I begin to say, but Mari's exclamation drowns me out.

"*Seriously?* Are you freaking kidding me? You never got the alarm system activated? Are you *crazy*, Bri?"

I glance at her, cringe at her furious expression, then turn to speak to Detective Tucker and notice he is mirroring her angry stare.

I hunch my shoulders.

"First thing in the morning," I mutter. "I promise."

"*Tonight*, Ms. Cerver," Tucker retorts. "I know a guy. Let me go clear your house right quick, and I'll call him."

He steps away, shaking his head, and unlocks my front door.

"Stay here and stay together. I'll be right back," he admonishes before he walks inside my house.

"Seriously, Bri?" Mari asks again, one eyebrow raised.

"Hey, it's just been texts and calls, so...."

"No, ma'am," she interrupts. "No, ma'am. No excuse, especially living by yourself."

The withering look that she sends me renders me mute. It is only a few minutes that pass before Tucker's voice ends Mari's silent rebuke, but it feels like an eternity.

"All clear, come on in."

We gather in my living room to await the arrival of the Cosantóirí LLC employee.

No words are spoken, but none need to be - because Mari is right. I should have had the alarm system activated from the moment I moved in here two years ago, and the fact that I did not makes me realize how lax I have become about my safety.

No shit, Sherlock. Especially with what happened back in...

NOPE. Do not say another word. I got it.

The chime of my doorbell launches me out of self-recrimination and off the sofa, but Detective Tucker shakes his head and stops my progress.

"I'll get it," he says, and strides with purpose out to the hallway to answer the front door. Mere moments later he escorts the new arrival into my living room, and my jaw drops wide open.

Allen Jones is standing in front of me, looking even better than the first time I saw him. The man I want and cannot have, the man that I am ashamed to admit frequently appears in my dreams, approaches me with his hand extended in greeting.

Mari nudges me with her elbow, and I snap my mouth closed.

"Ms. Cerver, it's nice to see you again, although I wish it were under different circumstances," Allen says in that deep, sexy drawl that makes my entire body heat up, and I feel a flush coming to my cheeks as I wonder precisely what different circumstances he would prefer.

Hello? Are you dense? He made it clear he was not interested, remember? Focus on the problem, please.

I clear my throat, determined to remain detached – and to avoid shaking his hand at all costs.

Can't let him touch me. I cannot afford to have another round of fireworks go off in front of Mari – she notices everything...

"Nice to see you again as well, Mr. Jones. May I ask why you're here, exactly?" I reply, crossing my arms in front of my chest.

A megawatt smile that shows off his dimples and a twinkle in his stunning blue-grey eyes precedes his response.

"You're the one that called my company for help, Ms. Cerver. You tell me."

Wait... what?

I blink rapidly and find my mouth is gaping open in surprise again.

***

Mari comes to my rescue by offering beverages, and I follow her to the kitchen. The moment we are out of earshot of the men the questions start.

"Is that *the guy*?" Mari stage-whispers at me as she starts the coffeepot.

"Yep," I confirm.

"Super dreamy. I can see why you're interested."

"*Was* interested, Mari. Past tense. *Was*."

"Oh, whatever. I saw the look on your face when he walked in and felt the heat between you two. If the cop and I had not been here, you two would be banging on your couch right now."

My eyes widen. "I'm sorry, what?"

Mari giggles. "You heard me. You've got it bad for that guy."

"I'm not doing this with you, Mar. He had a shot, he was an ass, he blew it. End of story. I don't care how... how..."

"Dreamy," she interjected.

"Sure. Dreamy. I don't care how dreamy he is, this is *not* happening."

"Don't fool yourself, Bri," is her parting shot as she fills a glass with ice and water, pours a cup of coffee, then motions her head toward the other room. "Come on, let's get back in there and see what Dreamy Man has to say."

I growl softly at her before I confiscate Tucker's coffee mug so that I can purposely focus on the guy in my living room that does *not* send my pulse skyrocketing.

CHAPTER TWENTY
Allen

Even surprise followed by confusion cannot mar Brielle's beauty, and I barely keep myself from closing the distance between us and embracing her.

Instead, I move to the coffee table in front of the couch and unpack my laptop.

"Let me get this fired up so I can take notes while we talk," I tell my audience, and all three nod their acknowledgement and move to take a seat.

It does not escape my notice that Brielle chooses the armchair placed the farthest distance from where I am setting up my impromptu workspace.

"Would anyone like something to drink? Coffee?" the other woman in the room asks, and I smile at her.

"I'll take some water, please."

Detective Tucker asks for coffee.

As her friend moves toward the kitchen Brielle stands suddenly.

"I'll come with you, Mari," she announces with a nervous tremor in her tone, and I witness a pointed glance pass between them before they leave the room.

Wonder what that's about...

I turn my attention to Tucker.

"How've you been, Adam?"

He shrugs. "Living the dream, Allen, as always. I take it you and Ms. Cerver have a history of some sort?"

"She was my realtor," I explain, and hope he leaves it at that.

"Uh huh," comes the response that lets me know I have fooled precisely no one at all.

The silence that descends is awkward, and it is only broken when Brielle and Mari return to the living room.

Mari marches over to me and hands me my water with a wink and a smile.

O...kay...

Meanwhile, Brielle's attention is completely focused on Tucker, and the feel of the room's atmosphere tells me that is by design.

Well then. Time to shift her attention to me.

"Start from the beginning, please, Ms. Cerver. When did the harassment start?"

"Six or eight weeks ago, I think?' she replies as she retakes the seat farthest from me. "A weird voicemail. At the time I figured it was a wrong number, so, I deleted it and forgot about it."

"What did the voicemail say, precisely?"

Brielle tilts her head back and closes her eyes, presumably searching her memory, and my hands falter on my keyboard as I picture myself kissing my way up that supple neck to nibble on a delicious-looking earlobe as I...

Down, boy. Not now.

"Ms. Cerver?"

"Sorry," she mumbles. "It was something like 'do you miss me' or something along that line. Not threatening, not even that weird, so like I said, I figured it was just a misdial."

"And approximately when was the next incident?"

We continue the questioning and I take detailed notes as to the increasingly aggressive content of the texts and voicemails she has received to date.

Escalating, I confirm as I skim my summary so far.

"Okay. This latest incident?'

She sighs, stands up, and approaches me long enough to hand me her cell phone so I can read it for myself. I fight to keep from clenching my fists when I see the clandestine picture taken of her earlier today.

"When we saw that, we called him," Mari chimes in, pointing at Tucker. "And he suggested it's time for Brielle to have some personal security in place. *Especially*" - her voice took on a matronly 'you're-in-deep-trouble' tone - "since she's been living here two years without any sort of home security system."

I almost chuckle at the dirty look Brielle shoots her friend's direction, but my concern for Brielle's safety ratchets up another notch.

"Well, that's easily remedied," I reply as I pull out my cell phone and dial.

"Pete," I say when he answers, "I need you to come to the address I'm about to text to you. Full setup, code two."

"You got it, boss," Pete says, and I hang up the call and send him Brielle's address.

Mari pins Brielle with a hard stare.

"You going to tell him the rest?"

"I don't think it's germane to the current situation," Brielle fires back, chin jutting out, steel in both her eyes and her tone.

"But it could be," Detective Tucker points out. "To protect you, he really does need to know all of it."

Brielle looks back and forth at the two of them before she hangs her head.

"Fine. But if we are going to do this, I need a drink. I'll be right back."

She stands and stomps back toward the kitchen.

CHAPTER TWENTY-ONE
Brielle

My hands are trembling so hard I almost drop the wineglass I've pulled out of the cabinet, and I take a moment to lean against the counter and focus on my breathing. When I feel steadier, I pour myself some Moscato, then mentally prepare myself to return to what increasingly feels like an interrogation room instead of my living room.

Don't be like that. They are trying to help you.

"I know," I mutter under my breath. "I just don't see how reliving it all will help. He's seven states away."

Allen really does need this information. You can do this.

I take one last deep, cleansing breath, straighten my shoulders, and walk back into the living room.

"Take good notes, because I'm not going to tell this story ever again if I can help it," I snarl at Allen as I move to sit down as far from him as possible again.

Mari comes over to me and takes my hand.

"If we didn't truly believe this will help him keep you safe, then we wouldn't ask it of you," she tells me gently, sympathy in her eyes. "And I am right here with you."

"I know," I assure her, and squeeze her hand before I take a large drink of my wine and begin to share an overview of my past.

"My real name is Becka Morgan, and I'm originally from New York. Fifteen years ago, I was in a relationship. To say it was not healthy is an understatement, but it took me a while to see that. He was very, very charming and hid his true nature for a long time. Once I realized what he was, I tried to leave, but he came home early that day."

My voice falters as a surge of memories that will never fade come to the forefront and threaten to drown me. I close my eyes, willing myself not to cry, and feel Mari's other arm circling my shoulders.

I draw in a deep, shaky breath as she murmurs, "You're doing great, Bri. "

I nod, a single tear escaping custody and coursing down my cheek as I take another deep breath and keep going.

"I refuse to get into the details but suffice to say that I had to have multiple surgeries to correct what he did to me, including some reconstruction work on my face."

I pause, take another huge drink of wine, and open my eyes, staring straight ahead and seeing nothing.

"The trial had to wait until I was healthy enough to testify, and I was scared brainless, but I did it. My ex is currently serving a twenty-year sentence in a maximum-security facility as a result. I found out later that I was not the first woman that tried to leave him - only the first *successful* one. Two other women disappeared and have never been seen again, but there's never been enough solid evidence found for the authorities to charge him in those cases."

Another large drink empties my glass, and I set it down on the little end table to my left and continue my story.

"Once the trial was over, I wanted to get as far away from there as possible. The only family I had left was my aunt and she lived down here, so, I contacted her, and she took me in and helped me get back on my feet. I changed my name legally and started my new life and tried my best to put all that behind me."

I risk a look at Allen, noticing his hands first, and am shocked to see his fists clenched so tightly that his knuckles are stark white. My gaze travels upward until it meets his, and the mix of empathy and rage I see there is making his blue-grey eyes almost glow.

I lean back and close my eyes, suddenly exhausted, and lapse into silence.

CHAPTER TWENTY-TWO
Allen

I have never wanted to rip another living thing apart with my bare hands - until now. The inhuman monster who terrorized Brielle deserves every single torture known to man and then some.

I watch her closely as I count down from two hundred in my head to try to calm myself before I speak. Her color is gone, her skin ghostly pale against her dark brown hair, and I witness her body go limp and loose with exhaustion from reliving what must have been the worst time of her life.

I fight the overwhelming urge to scoop her up in my arms and hold her close. Instead, I type a paragraph about what she just shared with me, and as I do, I decide.

I am not leaving her side until whoever is tormenting her is caught. Like it or not, Brielle Cerver is stuck with me twenty-four-seven until I know for sure that she is safe.

I am so much in my own head, plotting out arrangements, that I almost miss the question.

"Can you protect me?" she asks softly, almost a whisper. "Because I can't go through anything like that again."

I inject my feelings into my voice when I meet her gaze and answer her.

"You'll be safe with me. I promise."

She stares at me for several moments, then closes her eyes again.

"More wine?" Mari asks her, and Brielle nods.

The doorbell chime sounding startles us all, and it hurts my heart when Brielle jumps, then begins to shake.

"It's okay. It's probably Pete," I say, and head for the door.

My guess is correct. My IT specialist walks into the front foyer with two oversized equipment bags.

"You know what to do. I want this place wired up like it's Fort Knox," I tell him, and he grins.

"That's my specialty," he quips. "Where's the existing master panel?"

"Let's find out."

I lead him into the living room and introduce him to Brielle, Mari, and Detective Tucker. Brielle points down the hall in response to our question, and I walk with Pete to the master panel that is in the utility closet.

Pete glances at it and grimaces.

"What a piece of flea-market junk. Good thing I brought a full setup with me. I'm gonna replace this whole thing with something that will actually *work*."

"How long, you think?"

"If the wiring's decent, this should take two, maybe three hours, tops. And that includes the extra cameras installed."

"I'll leave you to it then."

By the time I return to the living room, Mari has refilled Brielle's wineglass and Detective Tucker is preparing to leave.

"I'll walk you out," I tell him, then say, "I'll be right back," to Mari and Brielle.

When Tucker and I get outside, he pauses.

"I looked up her case in New York," he says quietly. "With what he did to her, it's a miracle she lived, Allen."

"He still locked up?"

"That's the very first thing I checked. He got the maximum sentence of twenty years, no parole, so he will be locked up for seven more years. But I went ahead and set up an alert on his name anyway just in case some dumbass up there hits the wrong button in the computer system and accidentally lets him out."

"You read my mind. I planned on doing exactly that," I confide, but keep the rest of my thoughts concerning Brielle's ex private.

He ever sees the light of day again it won't be for very long. I will kill him myself.

Tucker shoots me a look that narrows my eyes. "What?"

He chuckles. "If I didn't *already* think something's going on between you and Ms. Cerver, tonight would have clinched it, for sure."

The sound of Mari clearing her throat behind me stops my sending back a cutting remark.

"What happens now?" she asks in a tone that leaves no doubt that she heard what Tucker just said.

"I'm staying with her," I respond immediately. "Round the clock, until we find and stop whoever's messing with her."

Mari arches an eyebrow.

"She won't like that. Come morning, she'll have her 'I'm bulletproof' attitude back in place, and she'll fight you on it."

"She can try," I retort before I can stop myself.

Mari gives me an appraising look.

"Oh, I like you," she decides. "You're going to be good for her, I can tell."

"Okay, then," Tucker interjects, seeming suddenly uncomfortable. "I'm going to head out."

"Can I catch a ride home, Detective?" Mari asks.

"Sure."

"Great, just let me grab my purse and tell Bri I'm leaving," she says, and darts back inside.

I notice Tucker gazing after her.

"Looks like I'm not the only one with something going on, maybe," I murmur, and he growls at me.

"Shut up," he mutters under his breath, then smiles as Mari rejoins us.

"Ready when you are, Detective," Mari announces. "Mr. Jones, it was nice to meet you, and I know you'll keep her safe."

"I will."

I'll defend her with my life, if necessary, I vow silently.

Mari leans forward and whispers, "I can see there's something special between you two. Just go slow and be patient. Give her some time to come around to it."

I remain silent, not sure exactly what to say to that, and she winks at me and follows Tucker to his sedan.

I watch them pull out of Brielle's driveway, then walk back inside to find Brielle still perched in her chair, wineglass in hand, with her head leaned back and her eyes closed.

I pull the coffee table closer to her and sit on its edge in front of her.

"I know that telling me all that wasn't easy on you," I say gently. "And I'm so sorry you went through that."

"Thanks," she whispers, then echoes Mari's inquiry. "What happens now?"

"What happens now is, Pete's revamping your security system, and until whoever is harassing you is caught, you have a roommate."

She opens her eyes and raises her head to stare at me, her green eyes alight with irritation.

"I'm sorry. What did you say?"

"Until the threat to your safety is resolved, I am staying here."

"*No.*"

"It's a notification, Brielle, not a request."

I stand, move the coffee table back to its original position, and head toward the front door.

"Where are you going? I thought you just said you were staying here?"

"And I am. But my ready bag is in the truck."

Her snidely muttered, "Great, just great," rings in my ears and I am unable to stifle a chuckle as I walk out to retrieve it.

CHAPTER TWENTY-THREE
Brielle

You have got to be kidding me, is all I can think when Allen announces that I have just grown a shadow. *Isn't that a bit drastic?*

But he's serious. I can tell by the look on his face that I will be lucky to go to the bathroom by myself until this is all over.

"Great, just great," I mumble when I realize I do not get a say, and I frown when I hear him laugh at me as he leaves the room.

Although I will never, ever admit it, it makes my heart do this weird double-thump thing to realize that for the foreseeable future, Allen Jones is a prominent fixture in my life.

I promptly frown again and push that feeling aside with all the force my tired psyche can muster.

The last thing I need right now is to pine after someone who is not interested.

I finish off my second glass of wine, then stand and carry the empty glass to the dishwasher.

"I'm heading for a soak," I say without preamble when I come back into the living room to see Allen standing there with a large duffel bag.

"Where can I put my things?" he asks.

"Spare bedroom is across the hall from mine. This way," I say, with the weariness I feel creeping into my tone.

He follows me down the hallway and I point to the door on our left.

"Thanks. I am going to go help Pete get your security setup in place. Just holler if you need anything," he says solemnly before he enters the guest room and puts his bag down on the bed.

I am too drained to respond, so I simply nod and enter my room, closing the door firmly behind me, and head straight into my bathroom to turn on the faucet.

I brush out then twist my hair up into a knot, fastening it in place with a hair band, before undressing and slipping down gratefully into the steaming water.

I soak, letting my mind drift, until the water turns tepid, then pull the plug and step out. I towel myself off and look longingly at my fluffy robe before deciding that since two men are in my house, more clothing is probably warranted.

I move to my dresser and retrieve underwear, a sports bra, my favorite sweatshirt, and yoga pants. Once I am dressed, I leave my room to go check the progress of my security system.

I find Pete and Allen standing just outside the utility closet, speaking in technical terms so complicated that it sounds like an entirely different language to me.

"You feeling better? Your color's back," Allen says with approval. "You looked a little pale before."

"I'm better. Just tired," I respond, then look away quickly before the raw emotion shining in his eyes saps my willpower completely.

"Have either of you had dinner yet?" I ask, trying to redirect my focus.

When they both admit they have not, I mention Chinese takeout. "It can be here in about a half-hour," I offer helpfully.

Two minutes later I am ordering my usual, plus an order of veggie lo mein for Pete and General Tso's chicken for Allen.

That done, I scroll to listen to the five new voicemails that I have received since I got home. I had put my phone on the charger in the kitchen and forgotten about it.

The first few words of the last one makes me gasp, and I blurt out, "Allen!"

He is by my side in an instant.

Trembling, I press the speaker button, then hit 'replay', and lock my gaze with Allen's as we listen to the latest verbal assault together.

The deep, raspy voice that has begun to haunt my sleep wastes no time in attacking, but this time the message is specific, and frightening in its intensity.

Two men tonight, huh? What a slut. But don't worry, soon the whole world will know all about you. I'll be seeing you real, real soon. Count on it.

Strangely enough, it is not the crude insult that gets to me. It is the fact that this stranger, this stalker, knows I am not home alone tonight - and there is only one way he could know that.

My knees give way and I almost hit the floor before Allen catches me.

"He's watching my house," I stammer, shaking so violently with fear that my teeth are chattering. "Allen... *he's watching my house....*".

CHAPTER TWENTY-FOUR
Allen

"Pete!" I yell as I cradle a distraught Brielle in my arms.

"Yes, boss," he says as he rounds the corner to join us in the kitchen. He stops short when he sees me sitting on the floor with a shaking Brielle in my lap, and his eyes flash with sympathy for her.

I thrust her cell phone into his hands.

"What time was the last call received?"

He checks. "About ten minutes ago."

"Bring Marlon and Mark in," I direct, my sharp, tense tone doing no justice at all to the white-hot rage surging through me. "I need them here as quickly and as quietly as possible. Read them in. Tell them that the perp's been watching the house. He could still be around, and if he is, I want him found. *Now*. Then see if you can trace that call."

"You got it," he intones, then glances again at Brielle with concern before he pivots and walks away, already pressing the button to get Mark on the phone.

I turn my attention to the obviously emotionally drained woman clutching at the front of my shirt.

"Brielle," I murmur, rubbing her back softly. "It's going to be okay."

"You don't know that," she whispers, her voice a thin tremor. "You can't guarantee that."

"Look at me. Brielle, look at me," I say, gently placing my hand under her chin and lifting her head so I can look into her eyes. "I've got you. Okay? And I'm not going to let anything happen to you."

Her mesmerizing green eyes brim with unshed tears before she lets her head fall forward to rest on my chest.

"Okay," she murmurs, her voice thick with tension. "Okay."

We sit a few minutes longer, her breathing slowly returning to normal, as I close my eyes and revel at the feel of her in my arms.

"I'm sorry," she manages to squeak out. "I probably should get off of you now."

I chuckle against her hair. "Honestly? I really don't mind it. You smell like vanilla."

I feel her face growing hot against my chest.

"It's my shampoo," she finally confides.

"Really?"

"Yes."

"Smells good. All the stuff for men smells like pine trees - or dirt."

That elicits a weak giggle from the captivating creature I am holding.

"You don't like smelling like the great outdoors - or a car freshener?"

I laugh out loud. "Woodsy? Not too bad. Smelling like floor cleaner or a Christmas tree? Not my favorite fragrance, no."

She laughs too, and the sound warms me.

We stay huddled together on the floor only a few moments longer before the spell is broken. Brielle wriggles out of my grasp and stands, then holds her hands out to help me up.

"Thanks," she says softly. "I'm glad you're here with me."

"I am too," I tell her earnestly. "Come on, let's go get an update from Pete. The sooner we get your system online, the better."

As we walk, she glances at me, her face scrunched into a confused look.

"What?"

"Did I hear you tell Pete to trace that call?"

"You did."

"But I thought those calls weren't traceable. At least that's what Detective Tucker said."

I smile. "For most people, they aren't. But we have much better toys at our disposal."

We round the corner into the living room to see Pete typing away furiously on his laptop.

"Just... about... got it..." he grunts at me. "Won't have any luck finding out who owns it if it's a disposable unit, but I'll be able to triangulate the phone's position at the time the call was made, at the very least."

"Really? You can do that?" Brielle asks him, and he gives her a gentle smile.

"Really truly. And it is accurate to within fifty yards or so."

My cell phone chirps at my hip, and I pick it up and read.

"Mark and Marlon are five minutes out," I announce before I text a response.

Full sweep, three-sixty, then come on in.

It takes mere seconds for *roger that* to appear on my screen, and I nod in satisfaction as I slide my phone back into its holster.

"Okay," Pete says as he presses 'enter' on his keyboard. "I also took the liberty of forwarding the relevant voice messages to myself so I can run them through analysis. I'm gonna let all that percolate while we set up the last four cameras."

He stands and moves swiftly, humming to himself, and leaves Brielle and me in the living room.

She looks at me and shrugs her shoulders.

"I really don't know what to do with myself at the moment," she confesses. "I need something to focus on other than that message."

"Well, we'll be another twenty minutes or so before the system's up and running. Have any other calls or emails to return? I can come get you when the food gets here."

She nods and turns to walk back down the hall. "I'll be in my home office."

I watch her walk out of sight, then move to join Pete.

"Anything you need me to do?" I ask.

"Yep," he says, shoving two cameras at me. "Backyard has blank spots that need to be corrected. There are existing cameras back there, but, well, they suck. These will cover the whole thing."

"On it," I say.

CHAPTER TWENTY-FIVE
Brielle

I sit behind my desk and turn on the little lamp that provides just enough light to properly see my keyboard and mouse. When I open my business email account, I see thirty-two new unread messages waiting for me.

Sighing, I scroll to the bottom and start with the oldest one first. Several of them are those annoying junk messages that always seem to outsmart my spam filter.

Those hit the trash bin immediately.

Several others are new possible clients reaching out, and most of them are worded very similarly - *I got your name from so-and-so*, etc. Those I respond to with an initial outreach mail template that I have perfected over time.

Still others fall into the 'current client' category; I have four that I am dealing with presently, one of which is the client that is stubbornly hanging on to the idea of winning the bidding war on that warehouse. I don't feel emotionally equipped to dive into that one tonight, so I mark it with a follow-up flag, open my calendar and set a reminder for tomorrow morning, and keep going.

***

By the time Allen comes to tell me the Chinese food has arrived, I only have seven new emails left to review. I push back from the desk and follow him to the kitchen.

We fill our plates and take seats around the kitchen table, with Pete setting a mini tablet next to him.

"This is the remote control for your system," he tells me as he points to it. "I'll walk you through all the bells and whistles after we eat."

Dinner talk is kept carefully devoid of my current situation, because I make a point of asking Pete about himself.

"Well, let's see," he says with a grin. "I'm originally from Orlando, joined the Navy right out of high school, retired after twenty years, and here I am."

"What did you do in the Navy?" I ask.

"Tons of things," he says mysteriously but does not elaborate further.

"Um... okay. Allen, what about you?"

"Born and raised in south Texas," Allen replies. "I also went into the military right after high school, but I went Army. I'd planned to stay until retirement, but things happened, and I got out after sixteen years."

The haunted shadows in his eyes fill my head with questions, but his sudden stiff posture warns me that asking them is probably not the best idea.

Allen's phone chimes and breaks the tension that's developed in the atmosphere all around us. He picks it up, glances at the screen, and grins.

"Calvary's here. I'll let them in," he says, and heads for the front door.

A few moments later, he is back, and standing with two of the tallest men I have ever seen, although at my all-time best height of five feet five inches, lots of people tower over me.

But these guys, particularly when Pete also stands up and joins them, form an intimidating wall of muscle. Not a one of them is under five-eleven by my estimation, and the two new arrivals look to be way closer to six foot four.

Not to mention every single one of them looks like they could bench-press my car, I think wryly to myself.

"Brielle, I'd like you to meet Mark and Marlon," Allen says, indicating each man as he speaks their names.

"Hi," I say, feeling very, very tiny but immensely protected at the moment.

"So, let's move to the living room and compare notes and decide on a battle plan," Allen says, then comes to me and extends his hand for me to join them.

CHAPTER TWENTY-SIX
Allen

I sit next to a solemn Brielle on the couch as my men take seats around the room. I tilt my head toward Mark as a sign for him to begin.

As usual, his reveal is short and to the point.

"Didn't see anything out of the ordinary, but then again we couldn't exactly go tramping around through her neighbors' backyards either," he tells me.

I notice motion to my left and swivel my head to look at Pete, who has grabbed his laptop and is typing something.

"*Finally*," he says on a sigh. "I was wondering how much longer that might take. Got a rough estimate of the caller's position when he left the message, boss."

"And that is?" I ask.

Two more keystrokes, and he looks up at me.

"Sixty-five yards due east of here."

"What, at the Andersen's house?" Brielle pipes up.

"That's what the triangulation is showing."

"But... but... they're *harmless,*" Brielle protests immediately. "They're both retired schoolteachers in their late seventies with hearts as big as the outdoors. She brings me cookies at Christmas time, for crying out loud. No way they are involved in this. No way."

"I'm sorry, Brielle, but the data doesn't lie," Pete replies as gently as he can.

"Your caller might very well have been on their property without them even knowing," Marlon chimes in. "I noticed what looked like a treehouse in their backyard."

Brielle nods her head. "They've lived here for years. They built that for their children, and now their grandkids play in it when they come over."

"My money's on the treehouse," Marlon says. "It's an elevated position, and nothing is blocking the view from it in this direction that I could see."

My gut agrees with his assessment, and I turn to the petite brunette sitting beside me.

"You think they'd let us take a look around?"

She shrugs. "Possibly. Only one way to find out. I can call and ask them. But what exactly should I say? I don't want to alarm them – or put them in danger."

"Tell them you've got a friend that's been considering installing a treehouse," I suggest, "and that you're wondering if he can come take a look at theirs to get some ideas."

Her brow furrows. "That could work – in daylight. Can this keep until tomorrow?"

"I don't see why not," I answer.

She nods and heads to the kitchen to grab her phone and make the call.

While she's gone, I look at my team.

"I'm thinking my being here is enough, for now," I decide aloud. "But Marlon, you're on standby."

"Got it, boss," he says as he and Mark rise to take their leave. "Anything comes up, I can be here in three minutes."

I walk them to the door and get back to the living room by the time Brielle returns.

"Marge said they'd be delighted to show you around," she announces with a smile. "We're expected at nine a.m."

"Good. Now, Pete, walk her through using that tablet, please."

***

Ten minutes later, once she is comfortable with operating the system via the mini tablet, Pete also shows her the two traditional keypads that he installed – one just inside her front door and one in her bedroom.

"That way you can still work the system if something happens to the tablet," he summarizes as I stand leaning against her open doorway watching the lesson.

"So, what? No buttons to activate any lasers?" Brielle teases and makes Pete chuckle.

"I didn't think you'd appreciate navigating laser beams if you have to get up in the middle of the night," he responds. "But I *did* install motion sensors inside the house that are pointed at the front and back doors, and they'll definitely trip if anything passes in front of either one while the alarm is set, so, keep that in mind."

"Right," Brielle answers calmly. "Anything else I need to know?"

Pete glances at me.

"Not for now," I say, "other than we need to talk about your schedule. I've moved my stuff around so I can go where you go."

She puts a hand on her hip as she tilts her head at me.

"You really think that's necessary?"

"Yes," Pete and I say in unison.

Pete and I head back to the living room, and he gathers up his bags to leave.

"You'll be monitoring?" I ask as I walk him out.

"Definitely. I set it up to stream live to my laptop in addition to recording it to our secure server," he confirms.

"Thanks, man."

"No problem, boss. Call if you need me."

I walk back inside the house to find Brielle on the couch, and I sit down next to her.

"Let's review the next few days, see what we're working with."

She pulls up the calendar on her phone.

"Let's see... we're looking at the treehouse at nine, and I have two showings tomorrow between eleven-thirty and two, but nothing the rest of the day. Sunday is free and clear, nowhere I have to be."

Brielle sets her phone on the coffee table, then leans back and looks at me.

"Now what? I know I should try to get some rest, but my mind is all over the place right now. There's no way I'd get any sleep."

"Me either," I admit.

"Wanna see if we can find a movie to watch?"

"Sure."

CHAPTER TWENTY-SEVEN
Brielle

When he admits he has never seen *The Cutting Edge* with Moira Kelly and D.B. Sweeney, I cannot help but grin.

"It's about this figure skater who needs a new partner, and she is a complete diva, and she's paired up with this ex-hockey player. I think you'll like it," I say, and Allen raises his eyebrows at me.

"All right," he says finally. "But I'm picking the next one."

"Fair enough," I tell him as I move to the DVD player and insert the disc. "Want any popcorn? Or a drink?"

"I'm sticking with water, for now, but I'll take some popcorn."

He comes with me to the kitchen and refills his glass while I make some popcorn in the microwave. A few minutes later we are settled in on my couch and I press 'play' on the remote control.

Allen's quiet through most of the movie, although he does laugh at a couple of scenes. As the ending credits begin to roll across the screen, I turn and look at him.

"Well? What did you think?"

"Lot less of a chick flick than I thought it'd be," he admits with a smile. "Not too bad."

"High praise, I suppose," I tease as I stand to take the empty bowl back to the kitchen. "Want to watch another one?"

"It's almost eleven," he reminds me. "Think you can sleep?"

"I can try," I answer, suddenly consumed with a burning desire to ask him one simple question.

He must see my conflicted emotions on my face because he suddenly asks, "What?"

Why were you such an ass to me the day we met? I want to ask, but I hesitate, because I am not sure I want to hear the answer.

Thinking someone thinks you are repulsive is bad enough. Verbal confirmation? No thank you, I tell myself as I mutter "never mind" and continue toward the kitchen.

But as I put the bowl in the dishwasher, then turn, I gasp, because Allen has followed me and is standing only inches from me.

"Something's on your mind. What is it?" he asks softly, his blue-grey eyes searching my face.

"I...um... nothing. It's nothing. I'm fine," I start to protest, but he steps closer, pinning me between himself and the kitchen counter. He puts his hands down on the counter on either side of me and leans forward until our lips are almost touching.

What is happening here? I thought he was not interested...

I feel my pulse kick into overdrive with anticipation.

"Brielle," he breathes, and then his lips are on mine, searching, pressing urgently, and the electricity between us fills the room with its intensity. His hands leave their stations on either side of me, and I revel in the feel of him touching me, one hand at the small of my back while the other fists in my hair. I moan, parting my lips, and his tongue takes advantage, thrusting forward to tangle with mine.

I run my hands up his arms and across his chest, delighting in the rock-hard muscles my fingertips are exploring, and when he breaks the kiss to trace a scorching-hot trail down my neck, I tilt my head to give him better access.

"Brielle," he says again, a reverent whisper that makes my knees weak. My body goes limp, and Allen responds by moving his hands to my waist and gracefully lifting me like I weigh nothing at all.

I am shaking again, but not from fear this time. My surge of need for this man is powerful and all-consuming.

The moment he sets me down on the counter, I move my knees apart so Allen can step between them, then wrap my arms around him to draw him even closer to me.

One strong but gentle hand slowly slides under my sweatshirt to caress my right breast, and I moan with pleasure.

Then, suddenly, it all stops. The next moment finds me both aroused and completely confused as Allen takes his hands off me and steps away, out of my grasp, his expression neutral, almost cold. The only remaining trace of the heat we just shared is a flash of fire in his eyes.

We stare at each other for what seems like hours, both slightly out of breath, before he speaks.

"You're a client," he manages. "I can't do this."

And without another word the man my entire body is crying out for turns on his heel and walks out of the room, leaving me embarrassed and alone.

I swallow hard, fighting back the tears that threaten to breach, and morosely hop down from the counter as I hear my front door open and close.

Work. Focus on that. It's helped before.

I scurry down the hall to my home office and close the door to avoid another humiliating encounter with Allen.

CHAPTER TWENTY-EIGHT
Allen

"Stupid, stupid, stupid," I mutter to myself as I make a trip around the perimeter of Brielle's home. "What was I thinking?"

The short answer? I wasn't. At least, not with the head I *should* be thinking with right now.

I sigh and run my hands through my hair in frustration as I remember the look on Brielle's face when I moved away from her - flush with a wild passion that turned to first confusion and then embarrassment before my very eyes.

And I am responsible for all of it. I want to kick myself.

Having satisfied myself that she is safe for now, I reluctantly head back inside. She's not in the living room or kitchen, and my instincts tell me that she is not willing to engage with me any further tonight.

Still, I need to confirm her location, so after checking her bedroom I head to the last place I can look. Her office door is shut but I can hear just enough noise that I know she's at her computer.

"I'm turning in," I call out to her through the closed door, and long moments pass before a terse "goodnight" makes its way back to me.

I wait another minute and it becomes clear that she is done speaking to me for the foreseeable future, so I retreat to the guest room and grab a few things from my ready bag to prepare for bed.

Not that sleep's coming anytime soon.

I have showered and am putting on pajama bottoms when I hear her footsteps coming down the hall toward my door, then her bedroom door closing. Next comes the sound of the alarm chirping as she activates it.

Glad one of us is staying focused, anyway.

I stretch my six-foot frame out on the bed and sigh, replaying the night's events in my head. My reverie is interrupted by my cell phone ringing.

"Hey, Pete," I say after I glance at the screen to see who is calling.

"Hey, boss," he says immediately. "Thought you should know that I got some prelim data on the voicemails. I think whoever is calling her is using a voice modulator. I'm still running some drill-down, and it's going to take a couple days to get it all analyzed."

"This just got more interesting," I muse aloud. "Increases the likelihood that it's someone she knows."

"Yep, that's my assessment, as well."

"Good work, Pete. Stay on it. I'll touch base in the morning once I've had a look at that treehouse."

"Roger that."

In the ensuing silence, my mind immediately reverts its focus to the woman across the hall from me, and I stare at the lazily spinning ceiling fan as I try to make sense of what I am feeling.

I have already cleared one self-imposed hurdle regarding Brielle Cerver – I want her. Badly. And I fully intend to do something about it.

Now, it is just a question of timing, but unfortunately, until the threat to her is dealt with, it will have to wait.

I am not sure exactly when my brain slows its pace enough to allow me to fall asleep.

What I *am* sure of is that the bloodcurdling scream I hear at three-ten a.m. has me up and moving across the room and across the hall in an instant.

CHAPTER TWENTY-NINE
Brielle

I have an inkling that it is going to be a restless night, even without what just happened between us in the kitchen. Reliving hell like I did earlier tonight always seems to make restful sleep impossible for me.

I wade through the seven emails I already had and am starting on the five new ones that just showed up when Allen's voice comes to me.

"I'm turning in," is all he says, and with the embarrassment I'm still feeling it takes everything I have to keep it civil and only respond with "goodnight."

I can sense him lingering for a moment before I hear him walk away from the door, and I breathe a sigh of relief, then return to my work.

After fifteen minutes, I shut my computer down and head for bed. I find myself pausing outside the guest room door before I turn and walk into my room instead.

I set the alarm from the keypad Pete so thoughtfully installed in my inner sanctum, then listen with satisfaction as it chirps through the sixty-second warning to fully armed.

Once I brush out my hair, I change my yoga pants, sweatshirt, and sports bra for a pair of old cotton shorts and a tank top, then crawl into bed and curl up on my left side facing the huge, empty expanse of mattress next to me. Only then do I unleash my mind and let it fill with the one topic that it has wanted to address for the last half-hour – the amazingly sexy but contradictory man right across the hall from me.

I close my eyes and replay what happened in my kitchen, an event that at the time I really hoped would come to its passion-filled conclusion right here in my bed.

Like a light switch, I realize. *From the moment we first spoke, he is on, then off again, with no warning at all when it's going to change. One minute, Allen is distant, like he hates me, and the next he's kissing me and running his hands all over me, and then, I'm just a client?*

So now what?

I punch my pillow in frustration.

I do not need any more drama in my life. I have survived so much already. I cannot take another round.

"But I want him," I whisper in the dark privacy of my room. "I want him."

I lie there, confused and hurt, for a long while before I drift off to sleep.

***

I grunt as I haul another box of my belongings out to my car, then check my watch.

One-thirty, I notice. Tony won't be home until four. I have plenty of time to finish loading up and get the hell out of here.

Still, I quicken my pace to pack up every available inch of space that I can in my four-door sedan. By the time I am done, only the driver's seat remains empty, and I'm covered in sweat.

It is a little after three when I go back through the house one last time to make sure I haven't forgotten anything, and when I come back out of the bedroom, I jump with fright.

He's home early.

***

Screams tear from my throat as I jolt myself awake, drenched in sweat, and I begin to struggle against the strong arms holding me.

"*No*," I sob, straining to fight back, break free. "No, Tony, no..."

"Brielle, come back, honey. You're safe, I've got you," is whispered in my ear over and over, and as I come to full consciousness I realize where I am.

When I finally muster the courage to open my eyes and look up, the lamp beside my bed illuminates the room enough that I see Allen's face mere inches from mine, his eyes filled with concern.

"Allen," I manage in a hoarse whisper, and cling to him as I begin to cry again.

"It's okay, baby. I've got you," he murmurs as he strokes my hair.

He holds me and comforts me as I cry the last of the nightmare out of my psyche, until at last the tears end and my breathing becomes less ragged.

"Thank you," I whisper, and receive a tender kiss to my right temple in response.

I feel him begin to pull away from me, and though part of me knows it is for the best, part of me is terrified to dream any more tonight.

"Stay with me," I find myself pleading, and the look on his face lets me know he is as surprised as I am by what I just said.

"Please," I whisper. "Just to sleep."

"Okay," Allen answers as he cups my face tenderly in his right hand.

He reaches out with his left hand to turn the light off, and I scoot over so he can climb into bed. I turn onto my left side and feel him moving closer until my back is snuggled, warm and safe, against his chest. He drapes his right arm over my waist, and I sigh as I relax into him.

With as long as it has been since someone slept beside me, I fully expect it to take a while before I am able to go back to sleep.

I am pondering the timeline when I drift off again, and this time, sleep is deep and restful.

CHAPTER THIRTY
Allen

Holding Brielle as she sleeps should not feel so good. So natural. So completely and utterly *right*.

But it does, and it takes my breath away to realize what that could mean.

I have not been this close to a woman in years – by design. But now, I feel this stirring deep in my chest, something I thought had left me forever when Mary did.

Protectiveness. Longing.

But it is much more than that. I feel... *complete* for the first time in a long, long time.

I tilt my head down to Brielle's hair and take in her soothing vanilla scent as I listen to her breathing become deep and even, and sleep overtakes me.

***

I wake sometime around sunrise, startled at first that I am not in my own bedroom. Then I feel Brielle sigh in my arms, and I look down.

At some point in the night, I rolled to my back, and she tucked into my side, one shapely leg and her left arm draped over me, her head on my chest. Her thin tank top leaves little to the imagination, and I picture myself stealthily scooting down the bed to capture one of her perfect nipples in my mouth. The result is an erection that I am positive she can feel pressing against her even as she sleeps.

I am torn between really needing to behave myself and wanting to shift her lithe little body on top of mine and wake her properly. When she sighs again, then begins to stretch and I feel her breasts rubbing against me, lust almost wins out.

Until her eyes snap open and Brielle recoils from me like I've shoved her.

"You okay?" I ask.

"Yeah," she mumbles, her cheeks going red. "I, um, forgot you were here, and it startled me. I haven't shared a bed with anyone in..."

"Years? Me either," I confess.

The look of disbelief that flits across her face almost makes me smile.

Almost.

"You hungry? I can make breakfast," I offer.

"What time is it?"

I glance over at the clock.

"Almost seven."

"Ugh," she laments, her face scrunching up to reflect her irritation, and now I do smile.

"Not a morning person, I take it?"

"Not without a shower and a gallon of coffee," she responds. "Speaking of which..."

She hesitates at first, then rolls away from me to the other side of the bed, gets up, and walks the long way around to get to her bathroom.

"Give me fifteen or so to wake up," she says as she stumbles along, her tiny shorts and top giving me even more naughty thoughts as I watch her breasts swaying with every step she takes.

"I'll have coffee waiting on you when you get out," I tell her, and am rewarded with a sleepy smile and a thumbs-up before she shuts the bathroom door.

And not only that, I tell myself as I get out of bed and turn off the security system, *hopefully by then the raging hard-on I've got will be gone, too.*

***

I will my body back to normal, but it only lasts until Brielle joins me in the kitchen twenty minutes later. The moment her scent reaches me, I am impossibly hard again. Fortunately, the jeans I chose for today's activities hide it a little bit better than a suit might.

"Feeling better?" I ask as I pull the rest of the bacon out of the pan and set it on a paper towel to drain.

"I am," she confirms as she takes her first sip of the coffee that I just poured out and handed to her. "But to be honest, I'd still be much happier if life could *not* start before ten a.m."

I chuckle at that. "Points for honesty. How do you like your eggs?"

"Hard scrambled," comes the answer as she takes a seat at the table.

"Want cheese on them?"

"Of course, I do," she replies with a smile. "Makes 'em even better."

"Coming right up."

Within a few minutes I am setting a plate down in front of her.

"Is that all right?"

"That looks fabulous. Thanks."

"No problem," I say, and carry my plate over to the table as well.

We eat in silence, but it is not a comfortable one, and I am dying to know what's running through that intelligent mind of hers.

"Brielle, about last night," I begin, and her shoulders hunch defensively.

"What about it?" Brielle asks, her even tone at odds with the tension emanating from her body.

"After the movie... you were going to ask me something, weren't you?"

She sighs and sets her fork down.

"I really don't think this is a good time to get into this," she mutters, then takes another sip of coffee.

"What are you so afraid of?"

She looks directly into my eyes and catches me completely off guard with her answer. "You."

"Me? You are afraid of *me*? Why?"

"Can we please talk about something else? Anything else?"

"No. I want to know what I've done that has you scared of me."

She closes her eyes.

"Not scared *of* you," she says in a small voice. "Scared by... you know what? I'm not doing this."

I reach out and take her hand. "Talk to me."

"Why, so you can confirm what I already know?"

"Huh?"

"I don't know what the hell happened between us last night," she says scornfully, "if it was a pity kiss, or whatever, but- "

I cut her off mid-sentence.

"A 'pity kiss'? You think I pinned you against the counter and kissed you because I feel *sorry* for you?"

"Well, yeah," she counters, her cheeks tinging pink.

"That is *so* not what happened."

"Isn't it?" she challenges, eyes flashing with heat as she yanks her hand back from me. "First, we talk on the phone, and I think there's a connection, then we meet in person and you are a complete asshole, like you don't want to have anything to do with me. And *then*, you show up at my house two months later and hold and kiss me, and then you haul ass out of the room. So, you need to tell me what the hell's going on here, because you are all over the place, Allen."

She leans back, arms folded over her chest, eyes still flashing, and waits.

"Fine," I growl. "You really want to know?"

"Yes," she retorts, jutting out her chin.

"I want you so badly I can't think straight, Brielle. I've wanted you since the first time I heard your voice."

CHAPTER THIRTY-ONE
Brielle

My jaw drops wide open at his admission.

"What?"

"That's right. From the very beginning. The moment I called your number and heard your voice, I wanted you."

"Wait, I don't understand... then why were you such a jerk that Saturday?"

I see his jaw clench. "Nothing to do with you. I was working through an issue. And in my defense, I did try to ask you out to dinner to make up for it, and you never returned my calls."

My ears go back at that little tidbit.

"Why would I return a call to someone that treated me so horribly the one and only time we were around each other?"

Allen drops his gaze.

"That's fair," he admits. "I don't blame you for not wanting to make contact after the way I behaved."

"So, if you've been attracted to me all this time, what stopped you last night?"

"Like I said, you're an active client of mine, Brielle, and that *has* to come first. I cannot keep you safe if I'm distracted, so until the danger is past, I have to stay focused on your protection, no matter what else I'm feeling."

I hesitate, then dive into the deep end headfirst.

"And what else are you feeling, exactly?"

The next thing I know, Allen is pulling me to my feet and crushing me against his chest.

"I want to strip you down and take you right here on this table," he growls in my ear and makes my center go instantly hot. "I want to explore every inch of you and feel your body shudder underneath me as I make you mine, for starters."

Trembling with desire, I slowly lift my head to look into his eyes and see the inferno from last night resurrected in full force.

"Allen, I..." my voice trails off.

"But I can't. Not yet. Not until whoever is threatening you is caught. Don't you understand?"

He wraps his arms around me, touching his lips to my hair, and I can feel his body shaking with restrained need as I slowly snake my arms around his waist and step into him.

We stand there, as close together as we can be, his heart pounding as hard under my cheek as mine is in my chest.

"So first, we'll deal with the threat. And after that, honey, prepare yourself, because you are all mine," he murmurs, his deep baritone doing delicious things to my core. I flush crimson as my imagination breathes life into all the seductive things this sensual man has just said to me.

"Guess we'd better catch them soon then, huh," I mumble against his chest, and feel the deep rumble of laughter vibrate throughout him before the sound leaves his throat.

"Count on it, baby. In the meantime," Allen says, squeezing then releasing me, "being that close to you is *severely* impacting my ability to keep my focus where it should be. So, let's sit down, finish our breakfast, and discuss meeting with your neighbors at nine."

I nod and retake my seat as he brings the coffeepot to the table and pours us each a fresh cup.

"By the way, I've been meaning to ask you – what does Cosantóirí stand for?"

"It's a nod to my ancestry," he explains with a proud smile as he sits down again. "My great-great-grandmother was full blood Irish. Cosantóirí means 'defenders' in Gaelic."

We finish breakfast, the mood lighter than before, and stand side-by-side at my double sinks to wash, dry, and put away our plates and silverware.

"We've got about an hour to kill," I tell him when I glance at the oven's built-in clock.

"I'm going to check in with Pete," he answers. "I'll be in the living room."

"And I'll be at my computer," I say before I head down the hall to my home office.

I leave the door open this time and sit down at my desk, pressing the power button to restart my computer. Once it boots up, I click on my email icon to open it.

What greets me turns my blood to ice.

"Allen!" I shout.

He rushes into the room, phone still to his ear, and glances at my screen, then motions to me not to touch anything else.

I stand and back away from my desk as he says, "Pete, get here as soon as you can, please. He's hacked her computer."

Allen hangs up the call and looks at me as I stare, wide-eyed, at the huge countdown in blood-red font in the center of my screen.

Seven days eleven hours twenty minutes forty-eight seconds… forty-seven… forty-six…

CHAPTER THIRTY-TWO
Allen

"You need to cancel your showings today," I tell her brusquely, "or get someone else to do them. You are not going. Matter of fact, I'm taking you somewhere safe until this bastard is caught."

"*No*, Allen. I have a responsibility to my clients to show up when I say I will."

"And *I* have the responsibility of keeping your stubborn ass alive and in one piece, Brielle. Don't make me *make* you put your own safety first," I snarl at her.

"What are you going to do? Tie me up and throw me over your shoulder?"

"If necessary, yes," I mutter through gritted teeth. "You might as well cooperate with me, because whether you like it or not, this is still happening."

Our scowling standoff finally ends when she snaps, "Okay, fine, whatever. I'll call Anne and see if she can cover for me."

"That's more like it," I say approvingly, and she flips me the bird as she waits for the other realtor to answer the phone.

"Anne, hi, it's Brielle. Remember what I was telling you about the other day? Yeah, it's escalated like you were worried about. I am supposed to meet the Martins and show them two houses today between eleven-thirty and two. Any way you can cover for me?"

She listens, nodding along with whatever Anne is telling her.

"Oh, that works out well then," Brielle says. "If you're going to be at both properties today anyway, I can just call Stan and Melody and explain that I can't make it and get them in touch with you."

She listens a bit longer, then finishes her call with "I really appreciate it... yes ma'am, I promise... okay. Thanks again, Anne, talk to you later."

"Okay, that's a load off my mind," she says with a small smile. "Let me tell the Martins the new plans right quick, and then I'll pack and come along quietly. Fair enough?"

"Fair enough."

***

Pete arrives within minutes, and I waste no time leading him back to show him Brielle's monitor and the ominous display.

"Got us a funny man, heh? We'll see about that," Pete intones, his ebony face set into a stony expression that belies his growing anger. "Gonna feel *so* good to nail this dude to the wall."

He swivels his gaze to me.

"You moving her?"

"Yep, and we'll be leaving right after the visit down the street to check out that treehouse."

"Off grid?"

"Completely. You got a burner phone?"

"You know it," he says, and pulls two items out of his bag to hand to me. "Brought you a fresh laptop, too. Encrypted."

"Thanks, Pete. Let me know what you find out about that," I conclude, pointing at the countdown message.

"Soon as I know, you'll know."

***

I stop in Brielle's open bedroom doorway just in time to see her tucking her cell phone into her purse.

"Leave that here. Laptop too."

"But... but... how am I supposed to..."

"You're not," I tell her. "Brielle, think for a minute. This guy has your number, and now, he's hacked into your home computer. What makes you think he can't track you via your cell phone or your laptop - if he hasn't been already?"

Realization dawns and her green eyes grow huge in an increasingly pale face.

I step forward and place my hands on her shoulders.

"Do you trust me, Brielle?"

She swallows hard. "Yes, Allen. I trust you."

"Then leave those here. Let's go meet with your neighbors, scope out that treehouse, and then we'll grab our bags and go."

I take her hand and lead her down the hall, pausing at her office.

"Pete, we're going to make contact two doors down. Be back in just a few."

"Roger that, boss," he says as he unpacks and sets up his own encrypted laptop.

CHAPTER THIRTY-THREE
Brielle

When I ring the doorbell two houses down from mine, Marge's beaming smile greets us as the door swings open.

"Brielle! Lovely to see you, dear," she says as she steps forward and envelops me in a hug.

"Hi Miss Marge. It's good to see you, too," I say earnestly as I hug her right back.

"Oh, my! Who's this handsome young fellow?" she immediately asks when she notices Allen standing behind me.

"Miss Marge, I'd like you to meet my friend, Allen Jones," I say, stifling a chuckle as she tucks her chin to peer over her horn-rimmed glasses at him.

"Nice to meet you, ma'am," he says, and when she extends her hand, he grasps it and kisses the back, making her titter with delight.

"Such a charmer, this one," Marge stage-whispers to me with an impish grin. "Hope you're gonna keep him around."

I flush scarlet and it's Allen's turn to chuckle as the little old lady promptly pivots and heads inside, beckoning to us to follow.

"Harold! Brielle's here!" she bellows as we walk into their living room.

"Brielle! Good to see you, young lady. Still wheeling and dealing in houses?"

"Yes, sir," I say, and walk over to where he's standing with his arms open for a hug.

"Harold, this is Allen, my friend," I tell him, and smile when I see that the once-over Allen's getting from Harold isn't nearly as friendly as the one from Marge.

"Nice to meet you, son. You doing right by our Bri?" Harold barks.

"Yes, sir, she's a special woman," Allen answers, his face serious.

"Good! Now, what's this about the treehouse?"

Allen smiles. "I'm thinking of building one, and I was wondering if I could get a closer look at the one you have in your back yard."

"Sure! Come on back. Ladder still's sturdy, but my knees won't take the climb anymore, so I'll just let you two go on up," Harold announces with a grin that makes me realize he's decided to play matchmaker.

We walk out onto their back porch, then across the lush green lawn to the spectacular oak tree that wears the treehouse proudly, like a precious jewel.

"Ladies first," Allen says, and holds out his hand in front of him.

I grin and quickly make my way up to the treehouse but am stopped short by what I see when I open the door. Some things – a lovingly worn small wooden table with two equally tiny wooden chairs and a narrow three-shelf bookcase – belong up here, as do the faded plastic army men strewn about the place.

Other things, like the expensive-looking binoculars and the sleeping bag, look brand new and very out of place – as do the large footprints clearly visible in the layer of dust that covers almost everything.

Allen climbs up right behind me and immediately pulls out his cellphone.

"Don't go inside or touch anything," he whispers so as not to alarm the sweet older couple waiting for us on the ground. "I need to take some pictures of this."

He solemnly does just that from the doorway. Then Allen works his way past me onto the little exterior balcony and maneuvers around to the west-facing side of the structure to poke his head through the open window and take more pictures of the interior.

"Act normal," he whispers when he returns to stand by me at the top of the ladder. "I don't want them to know about any of this until my team can get things under control."

I nod silently, suddenly fearful for the neighbors that have become more like family to me, and I use the climb down to get my game face back into place before I step to the ground and turn around to face Marge and Harold.

"Nice and sturdy," Allen remarks once he's back by my side. "How long has it been here?"

"Oh, about twenty-five years, give or take," Harold says proudly. "Built it for our boys. Then our babies grew up and had babies of their own and the grandkids used to come play in it. Course, they are almost teenagers now. Too cool to hang out in a tree when they can be playing video games these days."

We chat a few minutes more before Allen says, "Would you mind if a carpenter friend of mine comes over to take measurements this afternoon? I'd really appreciate it."

"That's no problem at all," Marge assures us. "We'd be happy to help."

After politely declining a meal, we make our way to the front door. Once we are outside again and walking back toward my house, the smile lighting up Allen's face fades.

"I'm going to get Marlon up there and see if he can lift any fingerprints. Hopefully, we'll get lucky."

"How's he going to do that without leaving more footprints? You saw how dusty it was up there. Whoever has been hiding out is going to notice if someone else walks around in there. And did you see those binoculars?"

"Not just binoculars," he reveals. "Extremely high dollar binoculars that no one in their right mind would just leave behind. Whoever stashed them there not only wasn't worried about them being taken, but they plan on coming back."

When his jaw twitches, I know he is holding something back.

"What? What else did you see?"

He shakes his head, and I stop walking and place my hand on his arm.

"Allen. You asked me to trust you, and I do, but that also means you cannot be keeping secrets from me. What else did you see?"

He sighs.

"Did you notice the little window facing your house?"

"Sure I did. What about it?"

"Did you see the floor underneath it?"

"No," I admit. "I couldn't from the doorway. The little table was blocking my view. Why?"

He turns his head and looks straight at me.

"There were three marks in the dust," he finally says after a long silence. "I think a tripod made them."

My brow furrows in confusion. "A tripod? Why in the world would someone have a tripod in a treehouse?"

He holds my gaze.

"Promise me you won't freak out," he murmurs.

"What?"

"Just... promise me."

"Okay, fine, I promise. Now answer the question – why in the hell would someone have a tripod up there?"

"For mounting a camera... or video equipment."

CHAPTER THIRTY-FOUR
Allen

"Oh. *Oh,*" Brielle's eyes widen at my announcement, and while I feel a bit guilty for not telling her what I'm *actually* worried about – namely, that a tripod can also be used to support a long-range weapon - I'm not about to mention it.

"But we can't rule it out either," she points out. "Not completely. You and I both know the messages are getting worse. Seems like video would be the next escalation."

Or sniper fire, I think grimly.

"Yes, they are getting progressively worse. And that is why we are leaving. I know you said Anne is covering for you today, and that you have nothing scheduled for tomorrow. But I think it's best that we plan to lie low for at least a week."

The color returns to her face as she stops walking again to argue with me. "Like hell. I have appointments and meetings booked all next week! I can't just bail on everybody, Allen."

"You can, and you will. You will call your receptionist - what's her name again? Rita?"

"Yes, but – "

"You're gonna call Rita when we get back to your house and tell her you're down with the flu, and that the doctor wants you to stay home and rest until next weekend."

That brings a flash of anger to her eyes, and she puts one hand on her hip and clenches the other into a fist with index finger extended to poke me in the chest.

She is adorable when she's mad, my brain blurts out all on its own, and I bite the inside of my cheek because I know that smiling is the worst possible thing I can do right now.

"Look, *buddy*, I was willing to humor you for a couple of days, but an entire week? Are you kidding me? If you are worried about some pervert videotaping me from the treehouse, then let's stay in a hotel so I can still do my job!"

I resist the sudden urge to grab her by the shoulders and shake some sense into her. The only thing that stops me is that I know she has not even considered what else could happen.

But she should. Being prepared for anything could save her life one day.

"Brielle," I say, all humor gone and a dangerous rasp of steel in my voice, "You may think it's okay to gamble with your safety, but I don't. I'd rather see you miss work and be pissed off at me, but safe, than see you stick to some damn schedule and end up hurt or worse."

That gets her attention, and she cocks her head to the side, narrowing her eyes.

"You're still not telling me something," she accuses, and I keep a stoic expression and do not reply.

She huffs and stomps away from me down the sidewalk, and I close my eyes and shake my head, counting down from twenty silently before I follow her.

The sound of tires squealing snaps me to attention, and I look up to see a dark panel van barreling down the usually quiet street. As I run to close the distance to Brielle, I see the van begin to angle, deliberately aiming for her on the sidewalk. She sees it and screams just as I tackle her, my momentum carrying the both of us out of the van's deadly path and causing us to land hard, then roll several times.

The driver guns the engine, the back tires throwing clumps of the neighbor's front lawn our direction as the van fishtails before finding some grip, then veers back onto the paved road and races past the Andersen's house and out of sight.

Brielle's come to rest on top of me, her head on my chest, and she is not moving. I roll her gently to her back onto the soft grass, and she groans, but her eyes open.

"God, Brielle! Brielle! Talk to me! Are you okay?" I ask as I run my hands over her and check for injuries.

"Winded," she finally gasps.

By this time Pete's running out of the house toward us.

"What the hell?" he yells.

"Tried to hit her," I say, a little short of breath myself from the hard roll we took.

"Plate?"

I shake my head. "Didn't see one. Call Detective Tucker."

As Pete makes the call, my attention immediately shifts back to Brielle.

"Let's... go... call.... Rita," she grunts, nodding her head as she looks up at me, her green eyes still wide and terrified as she struggles to catch her breath.

CHAPTER THIRTY-FIVE
Brielle

Once I am finally able to breathe properly again – and he is satisfied I have no injuries - Allen helps me up.

"Was that the kind of thing you're worried about?" I ask, and he just looks at me somberly.

"Okay, I get it now. The phone and laptop stay here. Anything else I should leave behind, just to be safe?"

"Your car. We're taking my truck."

"Fair enough."

I brush off my clothes as Allen reaches over and removes a small clump of dirt, beautiful green blades of grass still attached, from my hair.

"Do I have time to take a shower?"

"Yes - but make it quick. We need to get moving."

Pete hangs up from his phone call and announces, "Tucker's on the way."

The neighbor's front door slamming proceeds an extremely loud, "What the hell you think you're doing? Get off my lawn!"

"Good morning to you too, Mr. Patrick," I call out to the crotchety old fart that lives next door. "Someone just tried to run me over."

He shuffles quickly over to survey the damage to his yard.

"Dammit. I just got the Bermuda grass to come in nice and thick, too," he laments before he turns to me and gruffly asks, "You all right, girly?"

"A little shaken up, is all."

"Good. Did you see who it was?"

"A black panel van, limo tint on the side windows, didn't get a good look at the driver, and there was no license plate," Allen tells him. "We called it in."

Mr. Patrick looks at Allen, then at me, then back again.

"Well now. That sounds like the same van that was parked down the road from here a couple nights ago."

I can almost see Allen's ears perk up. "Where, exactly?"

"In front of the Crawford's place. About five houses that way and across the street," Mr. Patrick answers, motioning behind him with his thumb. "Old man Crawford was pissing and moaning about it because it partially blocked his driveway. He said he had to swing his truck out wide to get around the damn thing to head to work."

"Interesting," Allen murmurs, then turns to me and says, "You go get your shower. I'm going to visit with Mr. Patrick a bit more while I wait for Tucker."

I nod, still brushing what feels like a ton of dirt off my face and out of my hair as Pete and I retreat to my house.

***

Fifteen minutes later, I towel off and dress in a t-shirt and yoga pants - comfortable clothes for what could be a long car ride to wherever it is Allen's taking me.

Once my tennis shoes are tied, I stand up again and walk back into the bathroom to collect what I need to add to my suitcase – soap, shampoo, conditioner, deodorant, hairbrush, toothbrush, and toothpaste. After a brief pause, I double back and grab my hand lotion and some sunscreen as well.

The clothes I have packed are totally 'left-side-of-closet' items – jeans, yoga pants, t-shirts, and a hoodie, since I have no idea where we are going, but something tells me that hiding out is not going to involve fancy dress attire. I also grab my sleep shorts, tank top and my robe.

I place the items I have collected in the suitcase, then pick up my laptop and plug it in next to my bed.

No need to run the battery down, I reason with myself, although I still feel twitchy about having no means of communication with the outside world.

But as I close my eyes, the sudden image of the van lurching my direction is all it takes to make leaving my electronics behind a non-issue.

I don't think I have ever gone completely without them, though, I realize. *I've never fully 'unplugged', ever.*

This ought to be interesting.

In a flash of inspiration, I walk to my home office and grab four of the paperback books Mari loaned me – two romances by Erin Wright and two thriller stories by Paul Austin Ardoin. Pete glances up and smiles briefly before he returns his focus to my home computer.

I feel a twinge of guilt as I pick up the books, since I have been wanting to read them for months now, but never had the time.

But something tells me that whatever Allen has planned means I will have the time to get to them now, so I return to my room and add them to my suitcase before I zip it closed and hoist it off the bed to set it on the floor.

I extend the handle to its fullest height and wheel my suitcase out to the living room, then pull out my cell phone to call Rita and tell her an outright lie for the first time ever.

"Hello?"

"Hey, Rita," I begin, taking care to make my voice sound as weak and hoarse as possible.

"Bri! You sound horrible? Are you okay?"

"No," I croak. "Woke up feeling awful, so I went to the clinic this morning, and they said that it's a really nasty case of the flu. On bedrest for the next week."

"Wow, I'm so sorry you're sick. Need me to reschedule your appointments?"

"Yes, please," I say, feeling guilty for misleading her.

"You got it. Just get better, all right? And call me if you need anything."

I disconnect the call, carry my phone to its charger in the kitchen, and rejoin my suitcase in the living room to wait patiently for Allen to return.

CHAPTER THIRTY-SIX
Allen

"You're kidding," Tucker says as he looks at the torn-up lawn. "Didn't even slow down?"

"No hesitation at all," I confirm. "Straight up onto the sidewalk. If I had not knocked her out of the way, he'd have hit and probably killed her."

"Any idea how fast the van was moving?"

"No," I answer, my jaw ticking as I replay the scene over again in my head. "But the tires squealing is what got my attention first, so he definitely accelerated at the beginning."

Tucker makes notes on the little pad he pulls from his pocket as two uniformed officers measure fresh tire marks down the street.

"You're getting her out of here, right?"

"Just as soon as you and I are done talking," I assure him. "And you might want to talk to the next-door neighbor, and Mr. Crawford down the street. Seems that van was in the area earlier in the week."

Tucker's eyebrows raise as he makes another note.

"I'll do that, and we'll put out an APB on the van, as well. I have Marlon's and Pete's numbers if I need to touch base."

"That will work. Good hunting," I say, and shake his hand before I turn to go find Brielle so we can get on the road.

***

I find her sitting calmly on her couch, a suitcase at her feet.

"I called Rita," she offers, "and then I put my phone on the charger. It's in the kitchen."

"Good. Let me brief Pete, grab my bag, and we'll get going."

I walk down the hall to her home office where Pete has reestablished himself at her computer to continue to trace the countdown's origins.

"Bring Marlon in," I direct. "I want him looking more closely at that treehouse. Maybe we can pull a print or two. He's expected – I told them I'd be sending a carpenter friend by to take some detailed measurements."

At the confused look on his face, I mention the footprints and binoculars, and Pete's eyes widen in surprise.

"I recognized the brand. They are not ordinary binoculars, Pete, they are *infrared*. He can see everything, day or night, and there is a direct line of sight from the treehouse to this room," I conclude, then also mention the tripod marks as I move to the office's lone east-facing window and subtly close the blinds to at least partially obstruct anyone's view going forward.

"Closing the blinds won't help if the guy's got infrared and a sniper setup. Hell, before this morning I'd have called all that far-fetched, but now that she was almost run over, I think anything is possible at this point," Pete ruminates. "And if this guy decided to take a shot, her security system couldn't do a damn thing to prevent it."

"I know - which is why we're about to leave and stay gone for a week or so. You guys keep doing your thing and pass on any new intel."

"You got it."

I move to the guest room and grab my duffel bag, then return to Brielle still sitting patiently in the living room.

"Ready?"

"No," she admits on a sigh. "But I know it's the smart thing to do, so let's get moving."

***

After surreptitiously checking my truck for any sign of tampering, I guide Brielle to the front passenger seat and put our bags in the back seat.

We click our seat belts into place, then back out of her driveway.

"Where are we going?" she asks, her voice completely calm, like she wasn't almost mowed down in cold blood a half-hour ago.

"You'll see," I tell her. "Get comfortable. It's about a four-hour drive."

But not even a mile from Brielle's house, the shadow that we have grown becomes evident. A crappy, nondescript grey four-door sedan is keeping pace.

So much for heading straight to our destination.

I press a button on my steering wheel.

"Mark," I say when my team lead answers, "we have a tail. Need to switch cars. Can you meet?"

Brielle starts to turn her head to look behind us, but I put my hand on her arm to get her attention and shake my head.

She nods slightly to let me know she understands, then looks down at her hands twisting together nervously in her lap.

"Where you wanna meet and which one do you want?" Mark's voice comes to us through the speaker.

It only takes me a moment to decide.

"Parking garage at Fifth and Sycamore," I instruct, "and bring me the clunker."

Mark laughs. "Fifteen minutes?"

"That works. See you then."

Once I press the button to disconnect the call, I glance over at Brielle to find her staring at me, mouth open.

"You want to try to get away from whoever's chasing me in a *clunker*?"

I grin. "Just wait and see. I think you'll be surprised."

I play it cool, driving normally for ten more minutes. But once we get into the downtown area, I up the stakes. I push through a yellow light just before it turns red, leaving our would-be tail stuck waiting for another green.

I make two left turns, then a sharp right up into the parking garage, heading swiftly up to the fifth level.

"Here we are," I say, pulling in next to a white 1997 Dodge Caravan. "Our chariot awaits."

Brielle takes one look and snorts with laughter.

"You're joking, right? I can outrun that thing on foot."

"Don't let its appearance fool you," I tell her sternly as I grab our bags and toss them to Mark, who stashes them in the back of the Caravan.

Brielle walks around to the other side and starts to climb into the front passenger seat, but I stop her.

"Not yet. Get in the back until we're clear."

She rolls her eyes at me, but opens the back door and clambers in, settling in the middle row of seats.

I swap keys with Mark, who grins at the both of us.

"It's a gray four-door sedan, Texas plate," I tell him, then give him the number, and his grin grows wider.

"Well, I hope they're ready to see the *entire city* today," he announces with a chuckle. "See you later, boss."

I wave as he pulls away in my truck, then climb behind the wheel of the Caravan.

"So now what?"

"Now we wait for just a minute or two. Why? Are you ready to get started?" I ask Brielle, locking eyes with her through the rear-view mirror.

"As I will ever be," she retorts. "This ought to be interesting."

CHAPTER THIRTY-SEVEN
Brielle

Allen pauses, and I am about to ask what we are waiting around for when his cell phone chirps.

He swiftly reads the text, then lifts his head again to smile at me in the mirror.

"That was Mark. He has intercepted our shadow and is leading them away from us. It's safe for us to leave now."

Ah. That makes sense.

He backs the Caravan out of its parking space, and we begin the descent until we are back at street level, then turn left.

"Is it all right if I use your phone to call Mari?" I ask. "Just to let her know that we're getting out of town for a while. I don't want her to worry if she calls me and I don't answer."

He passes it back to me, and I dial my best friend's number. When she does not answer – Mari routinely ignores calls from numbers that she does not recognize – I leave her a message explaining that Allen is taking me somewhere safer for the next several days and not to worry.

"Thanks," I say as I hand him back his phone. "So how long until I can sit up front with you?"

"Let's at least get clear of the city limits first. Should be safe by then, all right?"

"All right," I say, and wince at the childish petulance that creeps into my voice.

Allen hears it too, because when I look ahead at his reflection in the rear-view mirror again his smirk is plain as day.

I roll my eyes, turn my head to look out the heavily tinted side window, and frown.

"Are these legal?" I ask, pointing at the windows. "I thought there was only so much tinting you could do."

"They skirt right along that cutoff but yes, they're legal, I assure you," Allen says with supreme confidence as he smoothly maneuvers the Caravan away from downtown and up onto the interstate.

***

We head south, the city fading into the distance, and Allen seems calm behind the wheel. I watch as he continually checks the van's mirrors, but we drive for a good half-hour before he takes an exit abruptly and stops at a gas pump in front of the tiny, dilapidated-looking convenience store located in the middle of nowhere.

"I would hate to break down out here," I mutter under my breath. There's nothing around."

Allen laughs. "I know, right? I have had the exact same thought myself. But the guy that runs this place is a friend of mine. We're safe here."
He pivots to look back at me.

"We need some gas and some snacks. We won't stop again until we reach the cabin, so, now would be a good time to use the bathroom as well."

With that, he climbs out of the minivan, gesturing to me to follow, and we walk side-by-side into the store.

"Bernie! How ya been?" Allen calls out, deepening his drawl as he speaks.

I flash a polite smile at the little old man behind the counter.

"Restroom, please?" I inquire, and he points a stubby finger toward the back of the tiny building before he extends his hand to my bodyguard.

"Allen! Long time no see."

The two men talk as I weave my way between steel shelves filled to overflowing with all sorts of junk food and find a surprisingly clean bathroom at the end of my journey.

I tend to business and wash my hands, then pull a hair band out of my purse along with my mini hairbrush and quickly tame my unfettered locks into submission. Feeling more presentable, I nod at my reflection, put the brush away, and walk back up to the counter, where Allen has just set an armful of things down and is paying for them.

Bernie bags our items and counts out Allen's change.

"Be careful, son," he intones with a wink and a grin.

"You too, Bernie. See you next trip."

When we walk back out to the minivan, Allen sets the bags in the floorboard behind the driver's seat where I will be able to reach them from the front passenger seat. I take up my new position as he pumps the gas he paid for, then gets behind the wheel again.

"Cabin, huh?" I ask.

"Yep. No one else even knows about it but me."

The smartass part of my personality seizes the chance to take over.

"*Ooh*. Do you need to blindfold me?" I purr, then laugh out loud as I see embarrassment, amusement, and lust all battle for position on Allen's face.

"Sorry," I giggle, tucking my head and covering my mouth with my hand. "Couldn't help myself."

But my giggle dies away in my throat when I turn my head to find Allen gazing intently at me, his eyes flashing with a heat that turns my insides to molten lava.

"Not for the ride down," he growls as he leans over to whisper in my ear, "but maybe I will once we arrive if you keep teasing me."

I gulp as I stare back at him, the promise of wanton ecstasy so clear in his expression that if he made a serious move right now, I would gladly crawl in the back seat with him in a heartbeat, regardless of being in public or not.

My cheeks flush scarlet as my imagination runs rampant, and he growls again.

"You're still my client, Brielle, but I'm not made of stone," he continues, then gently nibbles at my earlobe and makes me gasp before he retreats again and turns the key.

"Shall we?"

His voice is benign, almost too calm given that the inferno in his eyes has ratcheted up another notch.

Beet red and temporarily unable to speak, I can only nod as Allen pulls away from the tired old store and back onto the interstate again.

CHAPTER THIRTY-EIGHT
Allen

A great big clawfoot tub full of ice water, I find myself thinking as I drive. *Maybe* that *would make it go away.*

It is the raging lust that Brielle ignited in me the moment she mentioned being blindfolded in that sultry tone. It was all I could do not to drag her into the back of the minivan and take her right there in Bernie's parking lot.

Hell, it took all the self-control I possess to only touch her ear and *not* the rest of her.

My hands grip the steering wheel a little tighter.

Her safety comes first, I chant over and over in my head like a mantra. *Then we can move forward.*

But I can already tell I am going to need every bit of resolve at my disposal to keep the line between personal and professional in place until this is all over.

I risk a glance her direction to see that she has rolled down her window and is letting her right hand rise and fall, rise and fall with the wind. The flashback to the last time Mary rode in the car with me is painful in its intensity.

We ride along for almost an hour in complete silence, the atmosphere around us thick with tension, before Brielle speaks.

"Would you like something to eat? Breakfast was a while ago."

"Sure," I say, focused on keeping my tone neutral. "There's some peanut butter crackers in one of those bags."

She leans over, then back, and grunts in triumph. "Got them," Brielle says proudly as she tears open the multi-pack and hands me a package.

"Thanks," I say, and she shrugs.

"You're welcome," is all she answers before returning her attention to the scenery moving past us.

After several more minutes, Brielle clears her throat.

"Not that I don't enjoy crackers as much as the next woman," she begins, "but shouldn't we stop somewhere and buy some stuff for real meals?"

"Already handled. Pete placed an online order for me that should get us through the next three or four days. We just need to swing by and pick it up."

"Oh," she says, then hesitates, then blasts me with a question that I never saw coming.

"So, tell me again why nothing can happen between us? I would think that us getting... um, *closer*... would mean you would protect me even better. Emotional stake, and all that."

I feel my jaw drop even as I am shaking my head.

Please, no, I am hanging on by a thread as it is...

"You've already said it's not an attraction issue," Brielle continues softly. "So..."

"Honey, someone tried to hit you with a car this morning. I can't be as sharp as I need to be to keep you safe if I'm thinking about kissing you and stuff."

"*And stuff*? What are we, twelve?"

"You know what I mean, Brielle."

"I do," she fires back. "But I don't agree with it. The way I see it this should be a joint decision. You don't *get* to just choose celibacy for us unilaterally."

I feel myself start to cave.

"Brielle, I – "

"I'm not afraid anymore, Allen," she says softly. "Almost getting killed this morning brought everything into sharp relief. Believe me when I tell you, it's been years – *years* – since I've even been attracted to anyone after what Tony put me through."

I instinctively go silent and listen as I focus on the road ahead of us.

"And then, I met you," Brielle continues, "and it's felt like waking up again after a long nightmare. I know where I am, who I am, and what I want. And I want you. Life is short, and I have wasted the last fifteen years living alone like a shadow, Allen. I refuse to do that anymore."

She turns her torso in her seat to face me.

"So, my question to you is - are you in, or out?"

"It's not that simple," I try to tell her, but she raises her hand to stop me mid-sentence.

"Actually, it really is," Brielle says, her face and voice filled with embarrassment, "and it sounds like I just got my answer, so thanks for clearing that up for me."

With that, she shuts down, turning her entire body away from me to look out the passenger window.

CHAPTER THIRTY-NINE
Brielle

I turn as far away from him as I possibly can, unwilling to let him witness the raw pain of rejection filling my eyes.

Humiliating enough that I put myself out there and got stomped on, I lament in my head, even as I am fighting to keep tears from escaping and coursing down my cheeks. *But after the way he acted the day that we met I really should not have been surprised.*

I lean my head until it rests on the window that I just rolled up and watch the world outside pass by in a blur of misshapen colors.

That is, until I begin to feel seasick, and then I close my eyes and let the tears fall at will, making sure I stay silent.

Be rational for just a minute. He never said never, Bri, just not while you have someone stalking you. Don't you remember what he said to you in your kitchen?

I do, my wounded heart rails back silently against the logical voice in my head, *every word of it. But that sure as hell doesn't seem to matter much now, does it?*

When we stop in to pick up the groceries that Pete pre-ordered, I take advantage of Allen being distracted to move further back in the minivan again, if for no other reason than to physically distance myself from the amazing man who has just rejected me out of hand.

When Allen is finished stowing our food in the back, he retakes the driver's seat, then looks back at me. Fortunately, I have already wiped my face to rid myself of any tell-tale evidence of my mini meltdown.

Without a word, I lean my head back and close my eyes, shutting him out of my view. I hear him sigh, then start the engine, and the gentle sway as we get back on the road lulls me into a fitful sleep.

***

At some point, I become aware of a strong hand with a feather-light touch shaking my shoulder.

"We're here," he says, and I come awake with a start, my fight-or-flight instincts in full swing before I remember that I am in 'the clunker' with a man that once said he wanted me but evidently did not mean it.

I brush his hand aside and climb out of the minivan under my own power, then move to the rear to grab my suitcase with my left hand and three plastic grocery bag loops with my right.

"Lead the way," I tell him, and hate myself for the 'queen bitch of the universe' quality to my voice.

Allen raises his eyebrows but does not speak, moving ahead of me to unlock the door instead.

"You can have the bedroom, I'll take the couch," he mutters as he swings the door open for me then retreats to the Caravan to bring in the rest of the food.

I straighten my shoulders to mask my disappointment, set the three grocery bags on the counter, and head down the tiny hallway to the single bedroom in the place.

I dawdle for as long as I can, putting my clothes away in the dresser, until at last only my bathroom items are left. These I set on top of the dresser, reasoning that the bathroom probably has limited counter space.

You can do this, the primal self-preservation part of me that kicked in hard immediately after Tony comes slithering forward and whispers to me. *Just stuff it back down. No muss, no fuss. Quite simple, really - just slip your mask back on and keep going.*

But as I look in the mirror that hangs on the wall over the simple wooden chest of drawers and see my pale, drawn face staring back at me, I know the truth.

Allen Jones has awakened something in me that I thought had been destroyed all those years ago – hope - and nothing will ever be quite so simple again.

CHAPTER FORTY
Allen

I watch as she brushes past me to step into the cabin, no emotion on her face, before I turn to get the rest of the food unloaded and brought inside.

Nice work. You just blew it with her – again - even if you were *trying to make the right choices.*

"Dammit," I mumble to myself. "If she would just listen..."

I trail off, realizing what needs to happen, but hardly believing it. I need to come clean about the first time we met – be completely honest, about *all* of it - and hope that Brielle doesn't decide to walk away for good.

I carry the rest of the bags into the cabin and focus on putting our groceries away, letting my brain drift for a while.

When all the bags are empty and she still hasn't reappeared, I pull out my cell phone and check for messages.

There are two new ones.

Marlon was not able to pull any prints from the treehouse. Still working on voice analysis – Pete.

Dammit, I think to myself. *I need at least* something *about this case to move forward in a positive way.*

The one from Mark makes me laugh.

I think they got bored and went home! LOL.

I glance up at the closed bedroom door just down the little hall, and sigh.

Cook her something, pops into my head. *Brielle will at least come out of there long enough to eat, and maybe you can talk to her.*

A smile comes to my lips as I open the fridge again to retrieve what I need.

***

Forty minutes later, I am knocking on my own cabin's bedroom door.

"How do you like your steak?" I call out to her anyway when she ignores me and does not open the door.

"Medium well," Brielle finally answers, and I punch a fist up in the air because even hearing her voice again feels like a huge win.

The next twenty minutes or so I spend putting the finishing touches on the meal. I pull the casserole dish of au gratin potatoes out of the oven, then head back outside to flip the steaks.

When I come back in with the steaks, hers a perfect medium well and mine medium, I stop short. Brielle has ventured out into the open living room/kitchen combination and is watching me.

"It smells good in here," she admits in a casual tone that offsets the storm leaving shadows in the green eyes I adore.

"Have a seat," I gesture to the two-person table, and she does. I move her steak to a new plate, scoop up some potatoes to go along with it, and carry her meal and the salt and pepper over to her.

"Thanks," Brielle says listlessly, never taking her eyes off me.

"Something to drink?"

"Water's fine, thanks," I get in return, every syllable brimming with aloof detachment.

Once the glasses are on the table, I fill my plate and join her there. Silence reigns supreme as we eat, and when the plates are emptied again, I reach past mine to take her hand.

My heart flutters at the contact, and I know she feels it too when she gasps and blinks rapidly. But she does not shrink back from me, and I take that as a good sign.

"I haven't been honest with you about the first time we met," I say earnestly, and feel her body tense.

She closes her eyes and sighs, a deep exhale that underscores the exhaustion suddenly evident on her face.

"Allen, I really don't want to do this with you anymore."

"Just hear me out, Brielle. Please," I beg her, and wait until the tiniest nod from her gives me permission to continue.

"I used to be married. Her name was Mary, and she was my entire world," I reveal, and notice that Brielle has opened her eyes and is watching me again.

"What happened?"

"Cancer. She'd been sick but we didn't know why. Got the confirmation right before I was supposed to re-enlist for another tour. I left the Army to take care of her."

Brielle squeezes my hand but says nothing, her green eyes still watching me carefully.

"She made me promise that I would move on, find love again, and I did promise. It was the only thing she asked of me. But once she left me, I refused to honor that promise. I thought that it would be... disloyal," I explain, "and so for the last decade I've focused on work, and nothing else."

I quiet for a moment, steeling my nerves, then continue.

"Until I heard your voice, Brielle. And yeah, like you said in the car – it was like waking up again after a long, cold, dark, half-assed existence. After we talked that night, I went to your website and saw your picture, and it took my breath away. I was amazed at how much you resemble Mary."

I glance up from looking at her hand in mine to meet her gaze. Brielle's eyes are huge and round in her face, but full of understanding.

"Seeing me brought back bad memories," she murmurs quietly.

"Both good and bad," I confess, then swallow hard and press on. "And it scared the hell out of me – enough that I almost called you back to cancel our appointment. Because I have loved before, and she was ripped away from me. I was determined to keep my distance from you so that I did not have to face any of that. But now here we are, and I feel... God, *I feel again*... but it scares me to take that chance. Losing you would *already* gut me, Brielle, and that's just with us being brand new."

I stand, never letting go of her hand, and step around the table to drop to my knees by her chair.

"So, imagine the stakes if we get involved before I can catch this guy," I tell her softly. "*That's* the real reason why I've been hesitant about whatever this is between us. Does that explain it?"

A single tear trickles down her right cheek, and I reach out to wipe it away tenderly.

"Believe me when I say I want you - and not just sex, Brielle. If we do this, I am all in, one hundred percent, and I want the whole thing."

She raises her hand to caress my face.

"Not a single moment of time is guaranteed to us, Allen," she whispers. "And I don't want to spend one more second without you."

She slides out of her chair to meet me on the floor on her knees.

"So, let's stop fighting," she continues as she looks into my eyes. "Stop fighting this."

I gently pull the hand I am still holding toward me until her face is close enough to mine to kiss her.

The initial jolt of connection I felt the very first time I touched her to shake her hand that long-ago afternoon was surprising.

Last night in her kitchen, when I pinned her against the counter and kissed her, it was even stronger, making every cell of my body come alive.

Even reaching across the table just now to hold her hand caused a sizzling spark.

But all those times pale in comparison to the overwhelming surge racing through me when her lips meet mine as we kneel together on my tiny cabin's hardwood floor.

I know my life is about to irrevocably change.

All in, no going back.

I welcome it.

I walk to the edge of that cliff and step out on faith, believing, *knowing* that Brielle will catch me.

CHAPTER FORTY-ONE
Brielle

Still on my knees, I shuffle even closer to him so I can wrap both arms around him as he plunders my mouth, one strong hand at the back of my head and the other gripping me at the waist.

I feel Allen's heart pounding hard in his chest, echoing my own racing pulse, and I know that with this man is where I belong.

He wrenches his mouth away from mine, surprising me as he fists his hand into my ponytail and gently pulls down, tilting my head back so he can trace soft kisses down my neck, then around to my ear. His warm breath on my skin makes me shudder with anticipation.

"Bed," he murmurs against my earlobe right before he takes it between his teeth and nibbles.

I moan and nod, rendered speechless.

Almost before I am aware of what is happening, Allen lifts me off the floor and into his arms, and I wrap my legs around his waist as he pivots and carries me down the short hallway.

He sets me down gently on the side of the bed and kisses me again, this time slowly, sweetly, before he takes a step back.

"Brielle," he pants. "It's been a really, *really* long time – years - since I've... I don't even have anything with me to...I mean..."

I take a deep breath and bare my soul to him, the way he did for me earlier.

"It's been years for me too. But we don't need to worry about protection, Allen. I.... I can't have kids," I confess, hanging my head as I finally let go of my last dark secret that not even Mari is aware of. "That was another result of the attack. Hysterectomy."

"I'm so sorry," Allen says, leaning down to cup my face in his hands and rest his forehead against mine. "I'm so sorry, baby."

I close my hands around his wrists.

"It happened, and nothing can change it. But I can keep it from defining who I am," I tell him gently. "I just wanted you to know what you're getting into with me. Children are not possible."

"I want *you*, Brielle, just as you are," he responds, and kisses me again before asking, "You still want to do this?"

"Like you wouldn't believe," I tell him, and he laughs.

"What's so funny?"

"Remember the day we met at your office, and you asked if I was ready to go?"

"Vaguely. Why?"

"Because just seeing you standing there got me so worked up that when you asked me that, the first thing that popped into my mind to say was 'like you wouldn't believe'."

"That explains the growl I got, then," I tease him.

"Yeah. I was trying *not* to jump you right there in your lobby."

Another toe-curling kiss later, he stops and looks down at me with a twinkle in those stunning blue-grey eyes that I could lose myself in.

"That means there's only one problem left to solve," Allen says with a devious grin.

"What?"

"We both have on *way* too many clothes right now."

"Hmm," I purr as I take down my ponytail then lean back on my elbows and stick out my chest, "I bet we can find a solution to that pretty quickly."

I watch the twinkle explode into a raging fire as he reaches for his own t-shirt and pulls it off over his head.

Yes! Knew it. Washboard abs.

I sit up again and take off my own shirt, throwing it aside, then lean forward to unzip his jeans, but he takes my hands and closes the distance between us until I am lying flat on my back on the bed.

"Do me a favor and leave these here for a minute," Allen whispers in my ear as he gently lifts my arms so that they are resting above my head. "I got this."

His strong hands caress the sides of my face before traveling down my neck, then moving to my breasts, and I inhale sharply, lost in his touch. Next comes the gentle tug on the waistband of my yoga pants, and I lift my hips so that he can slide them down more easily.

Moments later my bra and underwear have joined my shirt and pants on the floor, and I watch, transfixed, as this perfect male specimen disrobes the rest of the way before he stretches out beside me.

"You're a goddess, Brielle," Allen murmurs, his voice deepening, as he gazes at my body. "Perfection. I want to nibble on every inch of you."

I feel my cheeks growing hot with his praise, then gasp and close my eyes as he leans his head down far enough to touch his lips to my left breast. As I begin to moan with pleasure, I can feel him shifting his weight, and I know that he is leaving my side to hover over me.

He teases me, first the left breast, then the right, with tender kisses and little nibbles before I feel his hot breath traveling down across my stomach. He marks his path with kisses, and each one only serves to fan the flames in me.

There is a brief but promise-filled pause as he moves down so that his shoulders are between my knees, and then he is tasting me, driving me higher and higher with every movement of his tongue. I cry out, clutching at first the bedsheets, then his hair, as Allen relentlessly explores me.

Just as I am about to crest, he withdraws, and I open my eyes to find him above me. I see the silent question in his eyes, and I cradle his face in my hands and answer.

"Make me yours," I whisper, and he rests his forehead against mine as he slowly slides himself home.

CHAPTER FORTY-TWO
Allen

The moment we are joined together, there is an outpouring of raw energy that passes between and through us. I go still for a moment, and Brielle shudders as I slide my arms under her to hold her close to me.

"You feel that too?" I whisper.

"Yes," Brielle gasps, running her hands down my back then gripping my hips to pull me as far into her as she can.

She moans, and I start to move, slowly at first, our eyes locked, watching each other as she meets my every thrust.

And when Brielle plants her feet on the bed, lifts her hips, and whispers, "take me there," I oblige, moving faster, harder, a guttural sound leaving my throat of its own accord. Time itself ceases to exist, the world fades away, and all I can see, hear, taste, smell, and feel is her in this moment.

She tenses under me, then cries out my name repeatedly as she explodes, her hips bucking against me, and I lower my head to her shoulder as I groan and follow her over the edge into oblivion.

***

After the euphoria has subsided, I lift my head to kiss her cheeks, forehead, mouth, then brush a strand of her beautiful brown hair aside.

"You okay?" I murmur, and Brielle sighs, her face still soft and dreamy.

"Fabulous," she purrs, softly running her nails down my back and causing my return to full mast. "You?"

"Baby," I growl against her mouth, "you keep doing that and we're gonna have to go again, right now."

"And that's a problem because…" she says, then shrieks when I roll us so that she is on top.

"You drive this time," I tell her, and she grins before she kisses me.

"Hold on tight, then."

***

Once we are both exhausted but sated, I leave her side only to draw a bath in the oversized clawfoot tub that I bought specifically for the cabin.

I return to the bedroom and scoop her into my arms, pausing at the dresser for her to grab her soap and shampoo bottles, then carry her in and set her down gently in the tub.

"Oh, that feels nice," Brielle says, closing her eyes and leaning back.

"Leave some room for me, baby," I tell her, then slide in behind her. I pick up the little plastic pitcher I stashed in the bathroom and use it to wet her hair when she tilts her head back. Then I pick up her shampoo and lather it in, massaging her scalp as I do.

"That feels so good," she moans unashamedly. "I nominate *you* to wash my hair from now on."

"I think I could be persuaded," I tell her before I lean forward to kiss her shoulder. "This stuff smells *so* much better than mine. Now, lean your head back again and let me rinse it out."

***

The bath takes a little longer than anticipated, mainly because we find it impossible to keep our hands off each other.

Rinsing the shampoo out of Brielle's long, gorgeous hair was one thing. Washing her body? Well, I got a little sidetracked but thoroughly enjoyed myself, and from the sounds I made her make, she did too.

"Hungry?" I ask after we are both dried off and she is wrapped up in her fluffy robe.

"Yes! And I feel like I burned a million calories recently. No idea why," Brielle answers, wriggling her eyebrows at me. "So yeah, I'm starved."

I laugh and swoop in for another kiss. "Bacon and eggs all right?"

"Works for me."

We move to the front room, where I walk over to my duffle bag to pull on pajama bottoms, then retrieve two saucepans from the cupboard and place them on the stove as Brielle grabs the package of bacon and the carton of eggs from the fridge.

"You handle the bacon. I'm making us an omelet," she announces.

"Deal."

I have just finished arranging the slices in the pan when my cell phone chirps. Brielle and I look at each other, then over at the little coffee table where I left my phone.

"Good Lord. Does he ever sleep?"

"What?"

"Two missed calls and a text, all from Pete," I tell her before I open and read the text message.

There's been a development. Call me please – Pete.

Brow furrowed, I dial and wait.

"Pete, what's going on?" I ask as soon as he answers.

"Boss, I did some digging," he says in a foreboding tone. "Did you know one of Brielle's current clients keeps some pretty shady company? Because I'm sure she has no clue."

"What do you mean?" I ask casually, not wanting to alarm Brielle, who is eyeing me from her position at the stove.

"I mean, I think he's mob-connected," Pete replies solemnly, and I close my eyes and pinch the bridge of my nose as I take this latest piece of news in and process it.

"Hang on a second," I tell him, then step outside to the porch where I can speak more freely.

CHAPTER FORTY-THREE
Brielle

I can tell by the stony expression on Allen's face that whatever Pete just told him was *not* happy news, despite the thumbs-up he gives me before he opens the door and walks out into the night air, shutting the door firmly behind him.

While he is gone, I tend the pan of bacon, rotating the pieces to make sure they cook evenly and do not burn. But I find myself smiling as the memories Allen and I have created tonight play like a carousel in my mind.

The first time we made love started off slow and sensual. The subsequent times took on different moods – playful, carnal – but every single one of them had one thing in common: a passionately deep and abiding emotional connection unlike anything I have ever experienced.

The mere thought of it makes me go deliciously warm from head to toe.

Humming to myself, I pull the cooked bacon from the pan and set them on a paper towel to drain, then turn my attention to prepping ingredients for the omelet. I have just about finished chopping up green onions and some ham when Allen comes back into the cabin and plugs in his phone.

He crosses the room and wraps his arms around me, snuggling against my back and resting his chin on my shoulder.

"Sorry I was gone so long," he murmurs.

"Is everything all right?" I ask, knowing full well that the answer could deflate the protective bubble of bliss that I am currently cocooned in thanks to the gorgeous man holding me.

He sighs.

"How well do you know Calvin Roberts?"

"My client? Not at all on any sort of personal level. But as his realtor, I know he has his heart set on owning this certain warehouse in Dallas, and that he is like a bulldog with a bone, he just will *not* let it go. To the point that he and some other parties are currently in a bidding war over it. Why?"

"Some information has come to light that leads us to believe he could have certain... people in his circle," Allen says, and I can feel my nose scrunch up in confusion.

I set the knife down and pivot in his arms so I can see his face.

"Huh? What people?"

"Mafia-type people," Allen answers, holding me a little closer, although I am not sure whether it is to give, or get, comfort.

"But what would any of that have to do with me?"

"I'm not sure," he admits, "but trust me when I say I plan to work this lead and make sure that it *doesn't* impact you."

"Okay," I tell him, and he releases me so I can throw the diced onions and ham into the saucepan. "Do what you have to do, of course. But I don't think that what is happening to me is connected to him at all. He was a client long before all this stuff started. The timing of it all doesn't line up, Allen."

"My gut says you're right, Brielle, but I have to rule it in or out."

"I know. And the sooner you do, the better, right?"

"Yep."

I add a touch of milk and a little bit of pepper to the four eggs I cracked open into a bowl earlier and stir the mixture briskly. Once the onions and ham begin to sizzle in the saucepan, I give them a stir before I pour the egg mixture into the pan as well.

"Spatula?"

Allen takes three steps to the right and pulls it out of the drawer to hand to me.

"Thanks. I'll need the shredded cheese, as well."

"Coming right up."

Within the next few minutes, I add the cheese in, then fold the omelet and turn off the burner.

"You don't seem very rattled by what I just told you," Allen observes as he pulls out two plates for us and puts some bacon on each one.

"That's because I know you're going to find and stop whoever it is," I tell him as I cut the omelet in half and add it to the plates, then set the spatula down and frame his face with my hands. "I *know* you will keep me safe. I believe that with all my heart. Now, how about we eat while it's still hot?"

CHAPTER FORTY-FOUR
Allen

Brielle never fails to surprise me.

I was hesitant to even *ask* her about Calvin Roberts, unsure how she would react, and unwilling to raise her stress level.

But she takes Pete's revelation even better than I did, and I feel her warm sincerity when she says she believes I will keep her safe.

With nothing more to discuss on that topic, I kiss her on the tip of her nose and sit down at the table to enjoy the meal she made. When we are finished eating, we wash and put away dishes, then snuggle up on the couch to watch a movie.

About a half-hour in, Brielle is fast asleep, her head on my shoulder. I stop the movie and turn off the TV with the remote, then angle myself so I can pick her up, bridal-style, and carry her to bed.

I walk back out to the living room to make sure the door is locked before I turn out the lights and join her. By the time I get back to the bedroom, she has awakened long enough to shed her robe and crawl under the covers.

I slip into bed and turn out the bedside lamp, then roll her direction to gather her to me in the dark. She sighs and moves closer, and I wrap my arms around her and rest, enjoying the way her body seems to naturally fit against mine.

These feelings are even stronger than I thought they would be, I admit to myself.

I touch my lips to her hair.

"I will keep you safe, Brielle," I whisper aloud in the pitch black. "No matter what it takes."

***

The next two days pass quietly, with no new intel about Brielle's case. Mark reaches out to let me know that he has paired Sam and Braeden up on a new assignment, and that the case Jack was working has been resolved.

Hope also reaches out via email about some accounting entries, and I review those over breakfast on Monday morning.

When we are not in bed, Brielle and I spend our time exploring the property using the two-person UTV that I keep stashed in the little shed behind the cabin. I bought the cabin, and the hundred acres it rests on, from my great-uncle years ago, and I love seeing Brielle's grin of delight as I drive her around and point out some of my favorite spots on the land.

The first question she has when she sees the pond is, "You have fish in there, right?"

I chuckle. "Yes, ma'am, that pond is very well stocked."

"I love to fish," she exclaims. "Haven't done it in forever."

"Well, then, I guess it's time we change that."

Fifteen minutes later we are back at the cabin to trade the UTV for the clunker and make a run into the nearest town for bait.

We argue good-naturedly about which bait is best as we travel – I prefer minnows while Brielle swears worms are better.

We end up getting both, and I notice the glowing smile she is wearing when we get back to the cabin and load up the UTV with two poles, the tackle box, and the bait.

I offer to set up her pole for her, but she declines, then surprises me yet again when she deftly adds the hook and sinker on the line, puts her worm on the hook, and casts her line out into the water. I rig up my line, add my minnow, then cast, and Brielle smirks at my shocked look when I notice she managed to cast hers out farther than I did.

My line is in the water for only a few minutes when she is already reeling hers in to land the first fish of the day, a gorgeous bass.

"Nice one!" I tell her as she proudly holds it up.

"Are we keeping or releasing?"

I shrug. "Depends. You want fish for dinner?"

"Absolutely," she says, and I rummage through the tackle box and get the stringer out.

***

Two hours later, I admit defeat. I have caught two keepers compared to her five, and we have enough on the stringer for a delicious meal.

"You're a natural," I tell her, and she grins. "No, seriously. My fault for assuming a city girl wouldn't know how to fish."

"I have a confession to make."

"What's that?"

"I'm originally from *upstate* New York, Allen. Plattsburgh, not New York City. I was pretty much raised on the waters of Lake Champlain. My dad and uncle were both avid fishermen, and they started teaching me when I was three."

"Holding out on me, huh?"

"Maybe just a little. Aren't you glad we didn't make any bets?"

"Very."

As we pack our gear back onto the UTV, I realize that there is so much more to Brielle Cerver than meets the eye, and I find myself looking forward to a lifetime of unraveling her mysteries.

I stop short and repeat one word in my head.

Lifetime.

Yeah. I am totally okay with that.

***

The morning of the third day starts the same as the last two – a slow, passion-filled merging of our bodies followed by a hot bath, then food.

We have just finished cleaning up breakfast dishes when my cell phone chirps.

I walk over and pick it up, and the hair on the back of my neck stands on end.

Call me. STAT. – Pete

With a knot of dread forming in my gut, I dial Pete's number.

"Boss," he says as soon as he picks up the phone, "Brielle doesn't have a stalker. She has *two*."

CHAPTER FORTY-FIVE
Brielle

I watch, concerned, as some of the color leeches from Allen's face and he grips the end of the counter for support.

"Say again?" he says sharply into the phone, then listens as he looks over at me.

"You're sure about this?"

Another long and foreboding silent pause as Pete speaks to him, and Allen runs his hand through his hair in frustration.

"Stay on it," he finally says. "Updates as soon as you have them."

When he sets his phone down and looks at me again, I can clearly see the worry in his eyes.

"What is it?" I ask quietly as I move to hold him.

"Voice analysis," he mutters. "There's a male that has been calling you."

"Yeah, well, we already knew that," I say with a smile, trying to lighten the mood.

"*And* a female, Brielle."

I feel my knees start to buckle a little.

"*What?*"

"Two different callers, one male, one female."

"What... how..." I begin, but words fail me as I try to make sense of what I am hearing.

"Voice modulators," Allen explains as he guides me to the couch to sit down. "People use them to alter the way they sound."

I frown, my mind racing, desperately wanting to believe that this is some sort of horrible joke.

"So..." I say slowly, "I have *two* people after me?"

"The voice analysis points that way, yes."

"This is starting to feel like a bad movie," I say, rubbing my hands over my face.

"Tell me about it."

But the more the news sinks in, the more pissed off I get.

"You know what?" I say as I stand up again. "I'm done. We're gonna end this."

"What? What do you mean?"

"I mean I'm done hiding," I announce, and Allen surges up off the couch to put his hands on my shoulders.

"We're not going back, Brielle. Not until – "

"*No*. I'm not going to abandon my life because two jackasses have some weird hang-up about me. The way we catch them is to meet them head-on," I snarl, then break contact with him and begin to pace the room, the seed of an idea growing bigger by the second.

"You can't be serious right now," Allen protests. "You're safest *here*, Brielle."

"And by staying here, cowering down in fear, I am letting them win," I counter, my voice beginning to rise in volume. "I didn't let Tony defeat me, and I am damn sure not gonna let *this* defeat me. They want a shot at me? Fine. Let's set the trap and watch them hang themselves."

The man I have fallen for looks at me, his jaw clenched so tightly that a tic has formed.

"You're not doing this," he growls.

"I'm a forty-year-old woman who can make her own decisions with or without your permission," I retort before I throw his own words back in his face. "You might as well cooperate with me, because whether you like it or not, this is still happening."

The corner of his mouth twitches upward as his blue-grey eyes change from showing anger to a surprised affection.

"You are the most stubborn, infuriating, pig-headed woman that I have ever met, you know that?"

"Which means I am a perfect match for you," I fire back, trying to suppress my own smile. "So, let's do this. Let's kick some ass and take some names."

CHAPTER FORTY-SIX
Allen

Seeing the woman that I have fallen head over heels for reach a 'pissed-off-to-her-core' level of mad is eye-opening, to say the least. I am a combat veteran, baptized more than once through mortar rounds and relentless gunfire, and even *I* would not tangle with her in her current state.

The very fact that Brielle wants to go on the offensive makes me almost feel sorry for whoever has been harassing her, because they have no idea of the pending hell that they have unwittingly unleashed upon themselves.

Almost.

I close the distance between us and take her hands in mine.

"Are you sure you want to do this?"

Her fierce gaze never leaves mine, and she never hesitates. "Yes."

"Then we will."

I retrieve my cell phone from the counter.

"Pete, we're coming back. Full team briefing in the morning, eight o'clock sharp, conference room."

A surprised Pete confirms my instructions and I hang up before he has a chance to ask questions.

"It's our last day here, then," I tell her. "What would you like to do?"

She lifts her chin.

"Let's head back out on the UTV, and you can teach me to shoot."

***

Within an hour it is obvious to me that Brielle Cerver is also naturally gifted when it comes to firearms. After I walk her through gun safety, loading and unloading, and sighting in, she steps to the line to take aim at the first of seven targets that are set up about ten feet away.

She chambers the first round in like I showed her, sights in, and fires, only missing the center of the target by a few inches.

"Not bad," I say. "Keep going."

By the time she runs three clips of ammo through the pistol, she is consistently hitting the center, with her shots clustered in an area a little bigger than a playing card.

"Are you *sure* you've never fired a handgun before? Because this is going kind of like our first fishing trip together did," I ask, and she laughs.

"Never in my life. Not doing too badly, huh?"

"Baby," I say, "I am beginning to think that there is nothing you cannot do. Now, switch things up a bit. I want you to try shooting left-handed, too."

She does as I ask, and while she is not quite as accurate left-handed, she is still good enough to be able to protect herself.

"Nice to know I can still defend myself if I can't use my right arm for some reason," she mentions casually as we inspect the grouping of the left-handed attempt.

The thought of Brielle being injured hits me like a punch straight to the gut.

"Hopefully, it won't come to you having to shoot to defend yourself at all," I tell her somberly, and she nods.

"I hope that too, babe, but just in case, it's good to have this skill."

"I agree. Now, let's work on shooting as you're moving."

***

We break for lunch, eating the sandwiches we packed earlier, then keep working on strengthening her skill set. As expected, her accuracy drops a bit during the run-and-shoot training, and Brielle is disappointed until I assure her that her marksmanship is still quite good.

"It's *always* more difficult to be accurate when you're running and shooting," I reveal, "no matter how experienced you are. For being brand new at this, you're excellent at it."

"Thanks," she says, and I can tell she is tired but proud of her accomplishments.

"How about we head back? We will be losing daylight soon anyway. I'll put some steaks on the grill and we can just relax."

She smiles as she makes sure that her weapon is empty of any rounds before ejecting the clip and carefully packing both pieces back into the case.

"Thank you," she tells me earnestly.

"For what?"

"Everything," she says simply, and leans over for a tender kiss.

***

We leave the cabin at around three-thirty on Wednesday morning, and I chuckle at the scowl on her face.

"I made you some coffee for the road," I offer as a means of apology for setting the meeting time at eight o'clock when our destination is a four-hour drive away.

Brielle grumbles but takes the travel mug and gives me a kiss on the cheek before she wheels her suitcase out to the back of the Caravan. I load it for her as she moves around to climb into the front passenger seat, yawning loudly in the pitch black.

"What about the rest of the food?" she asks me once I join her in the minivan.

"I moved what I could to the freezer, and what I thought we'd eat on the drive is in a cooler behind my seat," I tell her with an impish grin as I buckle my seat belt.

"I was completely wrong about us, Allen. We cannot be together. You are way, *way* too chipper this early in the morning," Brielle pouts.

She looks adorable, all sleepy and grumpy, and I laugh, lean over, and kiss her.

"Just wait until you realize that I can survive a long time on a ten-minute power nap," I tell her as I turn the ignition key.

"You're one of *those*? Ugh. Anything less than a two-hour nap just makes me angry," she proclaims with a frown.

I just smile and shake my head. "Drink your coffee, baby."

CHAPTER FORTY-SEVEN
Brielle

As the coffee Allen so thoughtfully provided begins to kick in, my mind clears of its cobwebs, and within the first hour of being on the road the caffeine propels me into a better mood.

Not that I want to always *be up before the crack of dawn,* I note sarcastically to myself. *This will* not *become a regular thing. No way.*

But with my brain beginning to function properly, I realize that in all my ranting yesterday I did not do one vitally important thing – think through exactly what kind of trap is necessary to lure in whoever is stalking me.

"Allen, do you have any ideas of how we're going to do this?" I ask. "Because I'll be honest, I am just now realizing I did not think that part through."

"I know. That is why we are meeting with my entire team, not just Pete and Marlon," he tells me. "Some of my guys have Special Ops training, and I think it would be good to get their input."

"Special Ops? Good to know. I bet they can come up with all sorts of cool things," I exclaim.

"They have to get... creative on occasion, yes," Allen confirms. "On *and* off the battlefield. Take the clunker here, for example."

"What about it?"

"This is no ordinary Caravan, Brielle. One of my guys, Braeden, is a hell of a mechanic, among other things, and he modified this thing nine ways to Sunday. Hellcat Hemi engine, bulletproof glass, armor plating in the doors, you name it."

"Shut the front door. *This* thing? *Really?*"

"Yep," Allen says proudly. "But she still looks like a normal minivan, honestly, and that is by design.

Excellent vehicle to use when you need to blend in and still be very much protected."

"Huh," I mutter. "I would have never known if you hadn't told me. The engine's not even that noisy for a Hellcat thingy."

"Thingy?" Allen arches an eyebrow at me and shoots me a playful smirk.

"Cut me some slack, I'm still not fully awake yet. But you know what I mean. If it has a bigger engine, shouldn't it be a lot louder? This thing is pretty quiet."

"Depends on the pipes."

"Pipes?" I repeat, confused.

"The exhaust system," he elaborates. "A lot of those really loud vehicles you come across sound that way because of the size of the muffler and exhaust system, not the engine."

"Huh," I say again, intrigued. "Learn something new every day, I guess. So, back to the original topic. Today is Wednesday, June the twenty-seventh, right?"

"Yes. Why?"

My eyes go wide as it dawns on me.

"I cannot *believe* I didn't realize it before!" I blurt out. "Allen, I think I know what that countdown on my computer was all about."

He looks over at me. "What?"

"The Realtors' Association banquet is happening on Saturday night at seven-thirty."

"I take it you planned on attending?"

"Yes, just like I do every year. With everything going on I completely forgot about it until just now. And I've had some issues syncing my calendar to my new phone, so it didn't show up when you asked me about my schedule for this week. You think whoever is after me is planning to attack me at the banquet?"

He does not answer me right away, and I can tell as I glance at him that he is lining out a plan in his head.

"Yes, I do," he says solemnly. "But that gives us an excellent starting point to focus on. Is it held at the same venue every year?"

"Usually, yes. But this year it's happening in one of the ballrooms of that new resort on Lake Grapevine."

"There's a notepad and pen in the glovebox," Allen tells me. "Get them out and take some notes for me. It will help us get the team up to speed faster during the meeting."

CHAPTER FORTY-EIGHT
Allen

"About how many people will be there?" I ask.

"In past years, they usually had round tables that seated nine people, and there were twenty tables, at least. But I've never been to the new place, Allen, so I'm not sure about the room size there."

I run some quick calculations in my head.

A hundred and eighty guests, minimum, plus figure anywhere from twenty to forty waitstaff and other hotel personnel. Conservatively, we are talking about trying to spring a trap surrounded by over two hundred and ten people without incurring any collateral damage.

Not to mention it probably has some sort of view of the lake, which means we need to assess the possibility of threats coming from the water....

Great.

"How do you feel about doing some reconnaissance with me after we talk to the team?"

"Sure. Where?"

"I want to get a first-hand look at the location. Maybe we can pretend to be engaged and tell them we're checking out reception venues."

Brielle bats her eyes at me. "Darling, I expected a proper proposal, at the very least."

I know she is teasing me, but the mere thought simultaneously makes my heart soar and my stomach tight.

Whoa there, buddy...

***

By the time the Dallas skyline appears in the distance, Brielle and I have lined out a solid base plan to share with my team, and I can tell by the excitement in her voice that she feels confident about catching her mystery stalkers.

While I don't want to curb her enthusiasm, my optimism is much more guarded, because I know all too well how things can go very wrong in a split second – particularly when the environment involves a large crowd.

I take the interstate exit that we need, and we pull into a parallel parking space in front of my office building at ten minutes to eight.

The group has already assembled, and Brielle smiles and nods when we walk into the conference room and I begin to introduce her to the team members that she has not already met – Braeden, my mechanic extraordinaire, Jack, Sam, and Hope.

When Sam stands up and comes over to shake her hand, I almost laugh at her response.

"Pleased to meet you. And please don't take this the wrong way, Sam, but I believe you just might be the tallest person I have ever seen."

The grin he gives her lights up his face. "No worries, I get that a lot."

Brielle takes in my team, then swivels her head to look at me. "It's almost like there is a minimum height requirement to be able to work here."

I shrug. "Never even noticed it, to be honest. I look at character, experience, and skill set. Besides, Hope's only what, five seven?"

"Five seven and a *half*, thank you very much," my accountant/office manager pipes up. "And I brought donuts. They're on the credenza."

We settle in around the conference table.

"Okay, here's what we have so far," I begin. "A series of voicemails and texts, starting about four months ago, that have progressed in frequency and intensity. Also, whoever this is hacked her home unit to display a countdown. Pete has been able to confirm that on at least one occasion the caller was located within seventy yards of Brielle's home."

I tilt my head Pete's direction for him to continue the narrative.

"Yes, one of the last calls she received before Allen hid her was from a neighbor's back yard," he confirms. "Allen visually confirmed evidence of an unknown individual using a treehouse two doors down to spy on her. But Marlon's search yielded no prints, not even on the infrared binoculars. Whoever is watching her is at least smart enough to glove up."

"They were *infrared*?" Brielle asks.

"Yes."

I can tell she has made the connection between the binoculars and what looked like tripod stand marks in the dust by the way she turns pale and darts her eyes quickly to me.

"You aren't worried about me being videotaped," she accuses quietly. "You think they are going to try to *shoot at me* from the treehouse."

The mood in the room turns even more somber.

"I believe that is a possibility, yes."

"So that's why I couldn't just stay home."

"Yes."

"Is it even safe to go back?"

I look at Pete.

"Brielle," he says gently, "five more messages came through while the two of you were gone."

She closes her eyes, but her voice is calm when she says, "What did they say?"

"I don't think that's important. What's important here is – "

"*Pete,*" she says firmly. "What did they say?"

He glances at me, and I nod.

"All about the same, actually," he tells us, his face devoid of expression. "But they got creative with the last one."

He taps a button on his laptop and the stalker's altered voice fills the room.

You can't hide forever. I'm coming for you. Nothing will stop me, and your screams as you die will sound like sweet music.

A long, heavy silence descends when Pete taps the button again to turn it off.

I look at Brielle, and she locks eyes with me.

"Well, then," she finally says, "I guess we had better make sure it doesn't come to that."

I reach over and take her hand.

"It won't," I promise solemnly, then turn my attention back to my team.

"Now, we think the countdown is in reference to the Realtors' Association dinner that's taking place Saturday night at the new hotel and conference center on Lake Grapevine. I want Mark and Sam to follow us out there later to look around. But first, I want to walk you all through some things that we brainstormed on our drive back and get your input."

***

Two hours later, after Brielle has traded her yoga pants out for jeans, she is beside me in the Caravan's front seat again and we are driving toward Lake Grapevine to scope out the location that I hope like hell results in a successful mission Saturday night. Mark and Sam are following behind in Mark's truck to check out the exterior layout, while my focus will be on the interior.

On Brielle's left hand is the stunning engagement ring that Hope loaned to us.

"From what I hear that place is ritzy, and you can't go there and pretend to be engaged without some sort of fabulous ring," Hope pointed out before she slid her own rings off and handed over her two-carat solitaire. "So here you go. Just take care of it. Jason will have my ass if something happens to that thing."

I immediately made a mental note to ask Hope later about the ring size when I noticed it fit perfectly on Brielle's finger.

CHAPTER FORTY-NINE
Brielle

The young twenty-something woman that greets us when we arrive at the hotel's front lobby is stunning, with long blonde hair and sultry blue eyes, and the way she looks at Allen – like he is some delectable treat just waiting to be tasted – makes me want to punch her right in the mouth.

You really wanna go there, little girl?

I can sense Allen's quietly amused discomfort, so I opt to squash little miss super-friendly's game right out of the gate.

"My fiancé and I are looking into venues for our wedding reception," I tell her with a smile, as I lightly stress the words *fiancé* and *wedding*.

When the flash in her eyes conveys that she sees my words as a challenge to be conquered, Allen's demeanor changes completely.

"And *she's* the love of my life," he tells her as he wraps an arm around my waist, "so I want our wedding to be as *perfect* as she is."

He proceeds to kiss me right in front of her until I am almost breathless, and when he is done, the look on her face – a disappointed resignation – is priceless.

"Now, young lady," he says condescendingly, "if we could take a tour, please, that would be most helpful."

"Yes sir, right this way," she responds, all business now, and I bite back a chuckle when Allen winks at me as if to say *you're welcome* the moment her back is turned.

She walks swiftly ahead of us as Allen and I stroll leisurely together, and he takes advantage of the distance to whisper, "I felt like a piece of meat just now."

"I could tell," I whisper back. "But don't worry, Allen. I wouldn't have let Miss Teen Queen anywhere near you."

"I'm pretty sure I have t-shirts in my closet that are older than her," he murmurs, trying his best not to laugh.

The young woman stops outside a set of double doors.

"This area, the Atrium, tends to be very popular for all sorts of gatherings, including receptions," she announces as she opens the doors and beckons to us to follow.

The room is spacious and elegant, a wide rectangle with subtle light cream walls and a gorgeous mahogany hardwood floor. But its signature feature is a long exterior wall composed entirely of thick glass that affords a spectacular view of the lake.

My eyes travel upward to see that the glass curves at the top of the wall, partially extending into the ceiling, as well, and as I walk across the room, I notice that even though the sun is overhead the room remains a comfortable temperature.

I mention that, and she smiles, her first genuine one for me since we met her.

"Yes. It can be a hundred degrees outside, and the Atrium will still hold a seventy-degree setting," she confirms. "I believe the glass is triple insulated, which helps maintain the temperature in here."

"What's the maximum occupancy?" Allen asks.

"The Atrium will comfortably hold three-hundred-fifty people, depending on the seating configuration," she tells us. "And the connected patio area is large enough for seventy more, should your guests require more room."

"It's stunning," I tell her. "What other sorts of functions do you typically see in here?"

"All sorts. Receptions, parties, conferences, training sessions. We even have a banquet coming up this weekend for the Realtors' Association."

Bingo.

We look around a bit more, and Allen pulls out his cell phone and takes pictures from multiple locations in the room.

"To help us figure out which area would work best as the dance floor," he explains when she gives him a puzzled look.

"Oh, certainly."

She gestures toward the double glass doors that lead out onto the patio, and we step outside and look at that area as well, with Allen taking even more pictures.

For a moment, I find myself lost in the fantasy.

"Allen, this place is perfect for us," I say as I squeeze his hand.

"I agree, darling. I just hope it's available the day we need it."

We follow our guide back inside, where she shows us three other locations on the hotel's property. Once the tour is complete, she hands us some brochures.

"I'd advise booking as soon as possible," she tells us. "Especially for the Atrium, as its calendar is filling up rapidly."

"How far out?"

"I can check and confirm for you, but if memory serves, it's already been reserved every weekend through next March."

Allen responds with, "Thanks so much for your time, we'll be in touch," and places his hand at the small of my back to escort me back out to the clunker.

Once we are out of earshot, he calls Mark.

CHAPTER FIFTY
Allen

"How is checking out the exterior going?" I ask the moment Mark answers.

"Well," he says, "the first thing we noticed was that wall of glass midway down the southern half of the structure. Was that the room in question?"

"Yes, our guide confirmed the banquet's scheduled to happen there."

"Interesting. There is a small land mass about five or six hundred yards off the shoreline, and it looks to be right across from that glass wall. Did you notice it?"

"I did, and I was thinking that it would be an ideal place from which to shoot a long-range weapon."

I sense Brielle's tension when I say that, and I put an arm around her shoulders.

"Yeah, Sam and I did too. Sam is in the process of renting a boat so we can get out there and take a closer look at it."

"Smart. Take lots of pictures. We'll meet back at the office at three."

"You got it."

I hang up and make another call.

"Pete, how's the research coming?"

"Already have a copy of the schematics for the hotel and a map of the lake."

"Good. We'll reconvene at three o'clock."

With that accomplished, I turn to Brielle.

"Since we're still not certain that your home is safe, I think you need to plan to stay with me at my place through Saturday night."

She considers, then nods. "All right. But I do need to at least swing by my house, otherwise I won't have anything to wear to the banquet."

"We can't risk it, Brielle. If your home is still under surveillance, we will grow another tail the moment we show up there."

She sighs. "I can't go to this thing in jeans, Allen, much as I'd like to."

"I bet we can figure something out," I offer. "How do you feel about shopping?"

She wrinkles her nose at me. "It's not my favorite pastime, honestly, but from the sound of it I may not have much choice."

"I have an idea. Hope's sister-in-law runs a boutique. I bet she'd be willing to meet us at the office."

"That could work. Speaking of Hope, I need to get this ring back to her. I've been mortified I'm going to misplace it."

"It looks good on you," I say quietly, and watch her nose crinkle up again, but this time the flush in her cheeks lets me know it's from embarrassment.

"Really? I don't know... I always envisioned something smaller, honestly. This thing is pretty, but it's huge."

Noted.

"Let me text Hope, and see if Bethany can meet with us," I say as I send a message.

It only takes a few minutes to get an answer.

She said she can stop by around five. Will that work?

Yes, I type back. *And while you two are working your magic, try to find out Brielle's favorite color, please.*

Hope's response takes only seconds.

What are you up to?

Will tell you later, I reply, then put my phone back in my holster.

"How about we get lunch while we're out here? I hear there's an excellent Italian place not far away."

***

By three p.m. the team has reassembled around the conference table. Braeden pulls down the wall screen so that Pete can project the lake map and the hotel schematics side-by-side for all to see.

"Pete, let's start with the hotel," I instruct, and moments later the blueprint fills the wall screen completely. I stand and move toward it with my laser pointer.

"The interior is pretty straightforward," I tell my team. "Meetings and conferences to the left, hotel guests to the right, and the middle section is the lobby, bar and restaurant area, with the employee-only areas – business offices, kitchen and so on – further back. This wide hallway to the left of the lobby area serves as the access points to the ballrooms. The Atrium is about halfway down the hall. Three sets of double doors that lead into the room."

"What's the room size?" Jack asks.

"According to our guide, depending on seat configuration this space can accommodate three-hundred-fifty people, with room for another seventy out on the separate patio that's connected to this room by one set of double doors."

"Pretty good size area," Marlon remarks.

"Yes, but what concerns me is that long glass wall. While it showcases a great view of the lake, it also creates some added points of vulnerability, in my opinion. The young woman we spoke with mentioned that the exterior glass is triple insulated to keep the room's temperature constant. What I *do not* know for sure is if the glass is also shatter-resistant, or if it would come completely apart if a round was fired through it. Speaking of which, I took the following photographs and emailed them to Pete. Pete, if you could please bring those up?"

"Sure."

"Allen, I can make some calls and try to find out what type of glass was installed," Jack offers. "A friend of mine owns the construction company that built that thing."

"Yes, please, as soon as possible," I answer, and he nods, then stands and leaves the room, pulling out his phone as he walks.

After pointing out a couple of things in the photographs I took, I turn the lead over to Mark.

"See this land mass here?" Mark points at one of the pictures I took facing the water from the patio. "That is a little island, about seven hundred yards from shore. Sam and I rented a fishing boat and went to investigate it. The whole thing is maybe two acres, max, but it has plenty of vegetation for cover – and it is located pretty much dead center across the water from that glass wall. Someone could dock a boat out of sight on the back side and work their way around to the shore-facing side with very few issues. And seven hundred yards is extremely feasible for taking *several* shots, not just one, especially if they use some sort of silencer."

Brielle swallows hard beside me, and I squeeze her hand just as Jack walks back in with a huge smile on his face.

"I think we just got lucky," he tells us. "My buddy just told me that entire wall was constructed using riot glass."

"Riot glass?" Brielle asks. "What does that mean? Like hurricane glass?"

"No, riot glass is even better," I say. "Hurricane glass is only rated for high winds. Riot glass is designed *specifically* to withstand objects hitting it – even something traveling at a high rate of speed."

"Like bullets?"

"Yep. The glass will spiderweb, but not shatter."

"And that's not common knowledge," Jack adds. "I would be willing to bet that our potential shooter thinks his rounds will penetrate that glass with no problem at all. We will increase our chances of catching him if we can slip someone onto that island at some point."

"Agreed," I say. "Who's up for it?"

"I'm in," Sam says with a grin. "Been a while since I've had a chance to play in the water."

"All right. We need to line out the rest of you for Saturday night. I will be attending the banquet with Brielle. Anyone have any ideas? I don't know how easy it will be to infiltrate the hotel's personnel for this without getting the police involved."

"Maybe we should," Brielle says quietly. "Detective Tucker's been very hands-on with my case, and I bet he could help us out with that part."

Within a few minutes I have him on the line and he agrees to come to the office.

***

About ten minutes after Tucker's arrival, Hope enters the conference room.

"Bethany's here," she announces. "I need to borrow Brielle, please."

"I'll be back in a little while," Brielle tells me with a smile as she rises to follow Hope out.

CHAPTER FIFTY-ONE
Brielle

As we walk, I slip off Hope's engagement ring and hand it back to her.

"Thanks for letting us use it," I tell her. "And I have to say, I was nervous the entire time about losing it."

She laughs. "I was too, at first. I could not believe Jason got it for me, and I was terrified to wear it anywhere because I just *knew* I was going to snag it on something somehow. But over time I got used to it, and now it feels really weird to be without it."

She slides off her wedding band long enough to put the engagement ring on, then puts her band on again.

"There. All better. Now, let's go see what Bethany brought. I gave her estimates of your height and dress sizes, and I am curious to see how close I got."

I follow her into a second, smaller conference room where a woman who looks to be about my age smiles warmly at me.

"It's nice to meet you, Brielle," she says. "I'm Bethany. I understand you have a formal event this Saturday evening."

"Yes, I do," I respond, "and unfortunately, I'm not able to access my wardrobe at the moment."

"No worries. I bet I have something that you will look fabulous in. I brought twelve dresses with me, all different styles. Shall we get started?"

***

We strike gold with the eighth one I try on, a chiffon and lace cocktail dress. Not only is it the perfect size, but the emerald-green color really brings out my eyes. The V-neckline and swooping cowl back are tastefully done, and the dress showcases my waist before it cascades into a soft, flowing skirt with an ankle-length handkerchief hemline.

"What do you think?" I ask Hope and Bethany when I step out of the ladies' room to show them.

"That's the one," Hope says immediately, and Bethany nods her agreement.

"I love it," I say, "and the hemline means I can wear several different heel heights. I'll take it, Bethany."

"Excellent," she replies, clapping her hands together with glee. "Let me take the others back out to the van. I'll be right back."

"See? That wasn't so bad," Hope teases, and I smile.

"I normally hate clothes shopping," I admit. "But Bethany has a way of putting people at ease. Once this is all over, I'm looking forward to browsing in her boutique and seeing what else I can find."

"Well, she carries everything from capri pants to full formal wear," Hope reveals. "And she knows her stuff. I'm sure you'll have a great time."

I return to the ladies' room and carefully remove the dress, hanging it up again before I pull on my clothes. When I return to the room, Bethany is back from her van, and asks, "What about shoes?"

I shrug. "I'll have to buy a pair."

"Do you trust my judgement?"

"Yes, I do."

"Then let me see what I can find. Size, and preferred heel height?"

"I wear a seven and a half, and I prefer three-inch heels or smaller."

"I'm on it," Bethany says with a smile. "I can swing back by here with them tomorrow, or I can meet you wherever you'd like."

"I appreciate it very much," I tell her, then turn to Hope.

"I probably ought to get back and see what the guys have come up with."

Hope nods. "I'll be there shortly. I'm going to walk Bethany out."

We part ways at the end of the hall, and I wave goodbye to the boutique owner before returning to the large conference room to get caught up on the plan.

But as I enter the room, it becomes clear that the planning session has wrapped up. Braeden, Sam, Jack, and Mark are gone, and Tucker is shaking Allen's hand.

"How much did I miss?" I say, trying to keep my tone light.

"The technical stuff. But we have everything lined out now," Allen responds as he and Tucker cross the room to meet me. "And we reached out to the hotel and read in their security manager. He's willing to let us place a couple of my guys in among his staff for the evening."

"So, it sounds like all that's left to do is wait."

"Yes. Well, besides get my hands on a tuxedo, that is," Allen says with a warm smile. "I haven't worn one in years."

Once Detective Tucker leaves, Allen glances at me.

"You ready to see my place?"

"I've seen it already. I was your realtor, remember?"

"Yes," he says with a grin, "but wait until you see what I'm doing with it."

Hope appears in the doorway and stops us.

"Allen, could I speak to you in my office for a moment?"

"Sure," he says, and squeezes my hand.

"I'll be right back, Brielle."

CHAPTER FIFTY-TWO
Allen

The moment I shut Hope's office door behind us, she starts in.

"Allen," she says in her best I-am-exasperated tone, "what are you doing? I've known you for over thirty years, and not *once* have I seen you mix business and personal, until now."

"I'm aware," I retort. "But she's different."

Hope sighs.

"Look. I get it. I really do," she says softly as she watches my expression. "I'm just worried about you."

"I know, and I appreciate it, Hope," I tell her. "But for the first time since Mary died, I feel whole again."

Her eyebrows raise. "That serious, huh."

"That serious."

She walks across the space to me and puts a hand on my arm.

"Then I am happy for you," Hope says, and the smile on her face tells me that her words are sincere.

"Are you done lecturing me?" I tease. "Because if so, I'd like to take Brielle home now."

"For now," she teases back, "but I reserve the right to invoke my privilege later, if needed."

"Yes, ma'am," I throw back along with a mock salute, then hug her.

"Thanks for being such a good friend to me," I murmur.

"You're welcome," she says as she pats my back. "Even if you are a supreme pain in my ass sometimes. Now, take your lady home."

***

I opt to keep the clunker in service due to its enhanced security features, and escort Brielle to the front passenger seat once we have said our goodbyes to Pete and Hope.

As we buckle in, I glance over at Brielle, who is watching me with a puzzled look on her face.

"What's the matter?"

"I have a question but I'm not sure how to ask it," she admits, and bites her lower lip.

"Just ask, and I will answer as best I can."

"Well... um... it's about Hope."

"Okay. What about her?"

"Are you two... you know... were you two ever involved, or anything?"

My face must reflect my surprise because Brielle grins.

"I take it that's a no."

"That's a great big fat hell no," I confirm. "Her big brother and I were best friends. Hope's always been the pesky little sister in my world, that's all."

Brielle frowns.

"But you're not best friends anymore?"

"We lost Keith in Afghanistan back in 2003."

She gasps, and her eyes go dark with sympathy. "I'm so sorry, Allen."

"He was a great guy, you'd have really liked him," I say, then change the subject. "But yeah, I have known Hope for a long, long time now. So long that it feels like we really *are* blood-related."

"I feel that way about Mari," she confides. "We only met ten years ago, but it's like she has always been a part of me. I don't know what I'd do without her."

"Good to have people like that in your circle."

"Yep, it really is," she agrees. "So now what?"

"My house, and dinner, for starters."

"You gonna fill me in on what I missed in the planning session?"

"If you like."

"Well of course I like. Might make me feel better knowing it all, since I'm the one that will have a target on her back Saturday night."

I put the clunker back in park and take both her hands in mine.

"I won't let anything happen to you. We're gonna catch this bastard," I tell her solemnly, and mean it with every fiber of my being. "I promise."

"I sure hope so," Brielle says with a nervous smile, "because the dress I picked out is fabulous and I'm gonna be really pissed off if it gets ruined."

I bring her left hand to my mouth to kiss the back of it.

"It won't. I swear it."

Her green eyes blaze with emotion as she looks at me and softly says, "I believe you."

CHAPTER FIFTY-THREE
Allen

Too soon, it seems, Saturday afternoon arrives. Hope stops by to drop off the tuxedo that I have rented, along with five different pairs of shoes for Brielle to try on.

"Bethany really does know her stuff," Brielle says as she looks at the selection. "Any of these will work."

"Told you so," Hope says with a smile. "I also brought the makeup you asked for."

"Guess I'd better go start getting ready, then," Brielle says, then hesitates, then flings her arms around a surprised Hope. "Thanks. For everything."

Brielle releases her, beams at me, then grabs the items Hope brought and heads into the master bedroom.

"I really do like her," Hope tells me softly.

"I'm glad. Your opinion matters to me."

Hope smiles. "Anything else you need?"

"Nope. I think we're good. Our guys onsite?"

"Jack and Mark are supposed to meet the security manager at six. Braeden will be working the valet parking and Marlon is posing as one of the waitstaff working the banquet. Sam's got his own plan lined out for getting onto that island, and Pete said to tell you he'll be monitoring it all from home base."

I chuckle when she mentions Sam. "Knowing Sam, he'll swim all the way out there so he can be even *more* stealthy."

"I'd say that is definitely within the realm of possibility. Have fun tonight, boss."

She stands on tiptoe to kiss my cheek before she leaves.

***

An hour later, Brielle appears in the living room, dressed and ready, and takes my breath away.

I swallow hard.

"You look... stunning. Amazing. Gorgeous," I stammer, and her cheeks and neck flush crimson.

"Glad you like it."

I slowly approach her, the long slender velvet box behind my back.

"There's just one thing missing," I say, and think *besides a diamond on that left hand telling the world you are spoken for.*

"And that would be?"

I bring the box into her line of sight. "I thought this might go nicely with your dress."

She takes the box from me and opens it, then lifts her head, eyes wide.

"Allen.... it's beautiful," she exclaims. "Where did you....?"

"Been in my family a while," I reveal as I lift the delicately spun gold and emerald necklace from its resting place to fasten it around her neck. "Hope mentioned your dress was green, and I thought this might go with it."

She kisses me tenderly before moving back into the master bathroom to look in the mirror.

"It's perfect," she says, a delicate hand coming up to her neck to gently splay across where the necklace touches her skin.

"Not as perfect as the woman wearing it," I say, coming behind her to wrap my arms around her waist and nibble on the earlobe that her elegant updo leaves exposed.

"You keep doing that and we are going to be very late," she purrs.

"Fine, I'll behave. Give me twenty minutes and I will be ready to go. But just know – the *moment* I get you back here, that dress is coming off."

She pivots in my arms and kisses me.

"I know," she murmurs, her voice a smokey growl. "I'm counting on it."

***

When we reach the hotel and take our place in line for valet parking, I insert my earpiece and check in with my team.

"Roll call. Everyone in place?" I murmur as Braeden, already completely in character as one of the attendants, strides toward the Caravan.

Five quiet rounds of *affirmative* plus a subtle nod from Braeden have me taking a deep breath and looking over at Brielle.

"Ready, darling?"

She shoots me a nervous look. "As I will ever be."

I step out of the vehicle to greet Braeden like I would a stranger, then swiftly move around to assist Brielle from her seat.

I tuck her arm into mine and can feel her trembling slightly as we quickly walk into the lobby, then turn left down the long hallway toward the Atrium.

"Listen to me," I murmur. "You don't have to do this. If at any time you change your mind, tell me, and we can go. My team will catch him, Brielle."

"No," she says quietly after a long pause. "I'm who he is here for. If I disappear, he will get suspicious, maybe bolt. This needs to end tonight."

We step through the first set of open double doors, and I witness Brielle's transformation from nervous target to self-confident career woman happen in an instant, like she has flipped a switch. She takes me around the room, the epitome of self-assured grace, and introduces me to some of her colleagues.

At seven-thirty, a delicate chime sounds, and people begin to look for their place cards to take their seats around the thirty eight-person tables placed strategically around the space. I notice that the table we have been assigned to lines up precisely with the patio doors – and that Brielle's assigned seat is *directly* in the line of sight out to the little island.

What are the odds of that? I think to myself sarcastically as I subtly switch place cards to put her in the seat to my right so that I am between her and the doors.

That accomplished, I pull out and hold her chair for her, then take my seat. Our attention shifts toward the west end of the rectangular room, where a small riser and microphone stand have been set up, and where a tall, slender man with salt-and-pepper hair addresses the crowd.

"Good evening everyone, nice to see you all here," he begins. "Welcome to the annual banquet of the Realtors' Association."

CHAPTER FIFTY-FOUR
Brielle

While I do not think it is obvious to any of our table's occupants but me, I can tell by the way Allen's body is angled that he is determined to remain a human shield for me.

I cut my eyes to his, but the tiny shake of his head tells me all I need to know – his senses are heightened based on the seating arrangement we stumbled into.

Of all the tables in the room, I try to tell him with my eyes.

I know. I've got this, is the reassuring sentiment I see when he holds my gaze, then squeezes my shoulder lightly.

With effort, I return my focus to the others at the table – Anne and her husband Benji, Lydia and her wife Sue, and another couple that I have never met.

"Hi, we're Dan and Matha Elkins," the woman says to me with a smile. "Originally from northern Utah. We relocated down here about a year ago."

"Hello and welcome," I find myself saying, and am glad that my tightly strung nerves are not overtaking my voice. "I hear Utah is beautiful."

"It is," Dan chimes in, "except for when blizzard season is underway. We like it much better down here."

With each passing moment I relax a bit more, and when the first course arrives, a wonderful-smelling Italian wedding soup, I beam at Marlon, who sets the bowl down in front of me with a flourish.

At one point, I glance to my right and notice Anne is watching both Allen and me. She subtly raises an eyebrow at me.

"Would you excuse me, please, I'll be right back," she says, and the look on her face I interpret as an invitation to join her.

Allen stands when we do, as do the other men at the table, and I can feel his eyes on me as I follow Anne out of the Atrium and toward the ladies' room.

***

The moment we step inside the bathroom, she turns to me, her brown eyes dark with worry.

"Something's up, I can tell. Why did your date switch the place cards?"

I falter. "Because we think there's going to be trouble tonight."

She taps her index finger against her bottom lip as I tell her about the countdown in blood red on my home computer.

"With everything that you have been going through, I can imagine being seated in line with the door liked that freaked you out. I am so glad we are at the same table, Brielle. I have my gun with me tonight, and so does Benji. You have our full support should anything happen, okay?"

I sigh in relief. "Thanks, Anne. That means a lot."

"You are most welcome. Now, tell me about the hottie you brought with you. You two look *great* together, young lady. How did you meet?"

***

When we return to the table Allen leans over and whispers, "Everything all right?"

"We have backup here, if we need it," I murmur into his ear.

He glances at Benji and Anne, who both give him an almost imperceptible nod of acknowledgement.

CHAPTER FIFTY-FIVE
Allen

The dinner plates are cleared away and the waiters, including a smiling, polite Marlon, begin to serve coffee and dessert.

I have just added sugar to my cup when Sam's voice comes through my earpiece in a faint but solemn whisper.

Target acquired. Wait one.

I glance at Marlon, standing across the table from me behind Anne, and his smile faltering for a split second lets me know he heard Sam's message as well.

Not much longer now, I think, and lean back slightly, mindful to keep myself positioned between the woman I love and the assailant that at this very moment is probably sighting in to try and kill her.

A brief swell of a breeze comes my direction from my left as a few banquet guests wander out onto the patio for an after-dinner smoke and leave the door propped open. Time seems to stand still for a moment, and I hold my breath as I notice a flurry of motion to my right.

I glance over and am horrified to see Brielle leaning forward to talk to the Elkins couple, and a green dot, shimmering at first, then becoming steady as it marks her skin just above where the necklace rests at the base of her throat.

Marlon has seen it as well, because his dashing around the table to tackle Brielle to the floor and shield her with his body is what caught my attention.

I rise from my chair with a bellow, pivoting to face the direction of the threat and leaning forward into the laser sight's beam as far as I can, and feel a red-hot burning trail in my flesh as the round meant for Brielle hits me full force - just past the edge of the bulletproof vest that I am wearing.

I got him, boss, I hear Sam say in my ear, and I nod weakly, the blood dripping down my arm turning the ivory tablecloth red as I try to push up, get to Brielle as screams of chaos echo throughout the room.

The hands that guide me down to the floor are firm but gentle.

"Hold still, Allen," Anne says, patting my hand as Marlon removes my tuxedo jacket and shirt. I hear a ripping sound and see Benji tearing strips of tablecloth with his pocketknife to pack both sides of the wound to try and slow the bleeding. "Paramedics are on the way."

I try to speak but cannot get words to form. As shock floods my system, my vision constricts, and when I look up again all I can see are the green eyes I adore, filled with tears.

"Don't leave me," Brielle pleads, but her words sound faint, distant, like I am underwater. I want to hold her, comfort her, but I am suddenly tired.

So tired.

Darkness takes me before I can tell her I love her.

CHAPTER FIFTY-SIX
Brielle

Within a half-hour of our arrival, Mari and Detective Tucker both show up, and I spend the next hour of my life with them, Anne, Benji, and Allen's entire team in the waiting room just off the hospital's surgical suites.

Sam sits off by himself in one corner of the room, brooding, his expression bleak. When I try to talk to him, he just shakes his head.

"I didn't move fast enough," is all he will say before he lapses into silence again, and I squeeze his hand before I honor his unspoken request for space and rejoin the rest of the team across the room.

I tuck myself between Mari and Anne, both of whom immediately reach out to hold my hands as a silent show of strength and support.

Mark returns from down the hall. "The waiter that was also hit is going to be fine. He's being treated and he will be kept overnight."

"Waiter? What waiter? I didn't know anyone else was hurt," I exclaim, my mind reeling.

"He was walking behind your chair when Allen was shot, honey," Anne tells me. "After it went through Allen, the bullet kept going and hit the young man in the forearm."

***

Two hours in, the lead surgeon finally appears to talk to us.

"He got lucky," he tells us. "Bullet missed all the vital arteries and nerve bundles, and only nicked a secondary blood vessel. I repaired it and as much of the tissue damage as I could. He will have decreased mobility for a while, and he will need some physical therapy due to the

trauma to the muscle tissue. But he should regain full use
of his right arm."

The tears I had held at bay flow freely as the man
speaks.

"Oh, thank God. When can we see him?" I ask.

"Another half-hour or so," he assures me. "Need to
get him into post-op. I will make sure someone comes out
to get you. No more than two at a time, for no more than
five minutes at a time."

***

"Now that we know for sure that Allen is going to be okay,
I'm heading to the station," Tucker tells us once the
surgeon leaves. "I need to go interrogate our suspect."

"Who is he?" I blurt out.

"Scott Bitzmore."

I feel my face drain of color and I glance over at
Anne, who looks as shocked as I feel.

"You know him?" Tucker asks.

"Yeah. He used to be a realtor. Lost his license a
couple of years ago. He is very strange. Always gave off a
weird vibe. He asked me out a couple of times, and I
always said no."

"For what it's worth, Brielle's not the only one who
thought he was creepy," Anne says firmly, her chin jutting
out. "Doesn't surprise me at all he'd be mixed up in
something like this."

"Interesting," Tucker answers as he scribbles some
notes on the little pad he always carries. "I'll keep you
posted."

***

My friends continue to hold my hands as we wait until
someone comes out to take me to Allen. After what seems
like a lifetime, a kind-faced woman in scrubs appears.

"First two, please," she beckons, and I look at the
group, then stand.

"Come on, girl," Hope says as she takes my arm. "You will feel better once you see for yourself that he is really going to be all right."

We walk side-by-side down the narrow hall, turning right and following the surgical nurse through a set of doors labeled "Post-Op Recovery".

"Bed two," she says warmly, and points. "I'll be back in five minutes."

I pause before I walk around the curtain, trying to brace myself for the worst. Instead, I am relieved to see that Allen is breathing on his own instead of still being intubated as I had feared.

I step forward, take his left hand with both of mine, and bring it to my lips to kiss it.

"I'm here, baby," I whisper. "I'm here."

He moans and turns his head toward me, his blue-grey eyes looking glassy and unfocused.

"Brielle," he breathes, and smiles in recognition before his lids flutter shut and he goes under again.

"Hey, boss," Hope murmurs as she moves to the right side of his bed. "How you feeling?"

"You get it?" he slurs, his eyes still closed. "Need to know that."

"No, not yet, but I will."

I raise an eyebrow, but she shakes her head at me and mouths *not now.*

"The doctor said you're going to be okay," I tell him, rubbing the back of the hand I am holding against my cheek. "And I am so grateful."

"Hurt," he moans, his brow furrowed as one of the machines monitoring his vitals begins to beep loudly.

A nurse joins us at his bedside. "Okay, Mr. Jones, no worries," she soothes as she presses a button feeding into his IV, and his face relaxes again.

"Everyone is here for you," I tell him as I put his hand down by his side. "So, I am going to let them come see you. I just wanted to make sure you are okay, and comfortable."

I lean over, kiss him tenderly on the lips, and speak from my heart.

"I love you, Allen," I whisper, then turn to go.

"Love you too, Bri," I hear him say before he snores lightly, and I smile through my tears.

***

I dig my heels in at first, refusing to even leave the hospital, until Mari and Anne finally talk some sense into me.

"Honey, he is stoned out of his mind right now on anesthesia and pain medications," Anne points out. "There is no point in you staying up here staring at him. He needs rest – and so do you."

"You know she's right, Bri," Mari chimes in. "Come on. Come back to my place, and we'll get some sleep, and we can come back up here first thing in the morning, all right?"

"Fine," I concede. "Pete, is it safe for me to go home to at least grab some clothes?"

Allen's men look at each other, then at me.

"We don't think so," Pete says as gently as he can. "You had *two* people calling you, remember? We have one guy in custody, and that is awesome. But we still don't have a clue who the female is."

"Do you have this person's voice on tape?" Anne asks, completely calm. "If so, let Brielle listen to it. It's not like she hasn't heard all the messages already, and besides, it should narrow your search pretty damn quickly if she recognizes the voice, don't you think?"

"That is an excellent idea," I proclaim. "Let's go do that first, and *then* I promise to go get some sleep."

Pete sighs. "Fine. Let's go."

Anne and Benji both stand and give me a big hug. "You need anything, young lady, you call us," Benji intones in his booming bass, and I nod.

***

Two hours later, I am slumped in my chair in Allen's conference room, frustrated in addition to emotionally and physically frayed.

"I have *no* idea who that is," I tell Pete and the rest of Allen's team. "No idea at all. I mean, it sounds vaguely familiar, but I don't know anyone from the Midwest. Maybe if I hear it again, I can – "

"Honey, we've listened to all of them nine times," Mari points out. "I think the best thing for you right now – for all of us, actually - is to get some sleep. You can always try again tomorrow."

"She's right," Mark says. "We can take you back to Allen's house and take turns keeping watch while you rest."

"Can Mari come with me? I don't want to be alone."

"You got it."

***

Mark leads the three-car convoy to Allen's house, and I stumble down the hallway to the master bedroom.
As I cross the threshold, Allen's words come back to me, and my eyes fill with tears again.

The moment I get you back here, that dress is coming off.

I sniffle as I make my way into the bathroom to hang up the dress and pull on my sleep clothes, letting the tears stream freely again as I scrub my face and take down my hair. By the time I crawl into Allen's king-sized bed and curl up on my side, clutching the pillow that smells like the man I love, I barely register that Mari is tucking me in.

I am so exhausted that sleep finds me in no time at all.

CHAPTER FIFTY-SEVEN
Brielle

All my life, waking up early has been the bane of my existence.

Until today.

I find myself sitting bolt upright in Allen's bed at six-twenty a.m., wide awake and ready to hurry back to the hospital to be by his side.

I power through a shower, throw on jeans and a t-shirt, and wrangle my wet hair into a messy bun before I add socks and tennis shoes to my look. The moment the second set of laces are tied, I am moving at a fast walk out of the bedroom and down the hall to the kitchen for some coffee.

Mari grins at me from behind the counter. "Well now, don't see *that* every day."

"What?" Braeden, our guard on duty, asks.

"She is up, dressed and in the kitchen, *and* it's before seven, *and* I didn't hear three different alarms go off."

"Smartass," I mutter as I pour myself a cup.

"Ah, *there's* the 'morning Bri' I know and love."

I ignore her and ask, "How soon can we get back up there?"

*****

When I walk into the private room that Allen was moved to sometime during the night, my heart leaps for joy. His color is much better, and the clarity of his gaze tells me the anesthesia has left his system.

"Hi, baby," he says with a lustful grin, and I color as the spectators in the room pointedly look anywhere else but at the two of us.

"Hi," I say softly, and close the distance between us to kiss him. "You really had me worried."

He attempts a shrug, then grimaces. "We got him, that's what counts."

"You're going to be okay, *that's* what counts," I correct him sternly, and I hear Tucker chuckling quietly across the room.

"Any updates, Detective?" I ask as I pull a chair up close enough on Allen's left side to be able to hold his hand.

"Bitzmore admitted to stalking you," Tucker says flatly. "He was the one in the treehouse, and in the van, and he left you roughly half of those messages. But he had no idea what I was talking about when I asked him who his female accomplice was. He seemed genuinely surprised."

"Why me?" I ask. "He lost his realtor's license over two years ago, and no one has seen or heard from him since. So, why me? And why now?"

"Good question," Tucker answers. "From what I gather, he holds you at least partly responsible for losing his license. Claims you 'ratted him out to the board', as he put it."

"That's absurd," I retort. "I didn't even know about the crap he'd pulled until *after* his license was revoked. I don't know how he got onto the board's radar, but it sure as hell wasn't me."

"Noted. Anyway, he says he was approached mysteriously about four months ago and offered a lot of money to, quote, 'make you sweat a little'."

"To what purpose?" Allen asks, his jaw clenched.

"He doesn't know. He just said he was paid fifty thousand to follow you and send you threatening texts and voicemails. Since he blames you for the whole license thing, he agreed to do it."

"Who hired him?"

Tucker sighs and runs a hand over his face. "That's the thing. He says he does not know. No names, and he never met anyone face-to-face. Everything was done through emails from dummy accounts and electronic funds transfers."

"Can't you trace the money?"

"We're working on it, but all that's going to take a few days, at least."

"What *I'd* like to know is where he learned to use a high-end sniper rifle," Pete interjects.

Tucker sighs again. "Bitzmore has military training. He got kicked out when they realized just how well he had managed to fake out the psych screening. As far as the gun? He says his phantom employer provided it – along with the promise of another two hundred thousand if he succeeded. We're working that angle too."

I look at Allen, then at the detective.

"So, what now? Can I go home, at least? Sounds like the threat of being shot at is past now."

"Are you nuts? *No*," Allen says immediately. "Someone was willing to pay Bitzmore a quarter of a million dollars to kill you, Brielle. There's nothing that says he was the only one hired for the job."

My temper finally gets the best of me, and I can feel my chin jut out in defiance when I retort, "Then I guess it's time to set another trap, isn't it? Only this time, at my house, not out in public. I don't want any more innocent bystanders getting hurt."

"I agree with Allen," Tucker says instantly. "That is a bad idea. Supremely bad."

"Good, then we're all agreed," I snap. "But it's happening anyway. Help me or stand aside."

"Could you guys give us a moment, please?" Allen says solemnly, and the room empties quickly.

"Not doing this, honey. No way in hell," he snarls the moment we are alone.

"It's not your decision."

He fists his left hand in his hair and tugs, his lips pulled back to show his gritted teeth.

"You are so....*frustrating*, Brielle," he manages to growl, and it is obvious that he is straining with the effort of holding back more colorful language. "Someone took a shot at you *just last night* in case you've forgotten. And now you just want to return to your house and play like it's all over?"

"To lure whoever is left and catch them so that I can get on with my life, yes."

"You're out of your mind," he grumbles. "Seriously."

I reach over, gently untangle his hand from the hair he is on the verge of pulling out and wrap my hand around his firmly.

"The alternative is to hide indefinitely and let some shadow-person dictate how I live the rest of my life. And to me, that is not living, Allen. That is barely existing. I already spent fifteen years barely existing, and I am *not* going back."

"There's got to be another way," he mutters unhappily, then pins me with a stare. "I can't lose you."

"You won't," I say with a bit more confidence than I actually feel, "because this will be on *my* turf this time."

A knock at the door interrupts us.

"Sorry, but there's been a development," Tucker says as he pokes his head in the doorway. "I need to get to the station. Don't decide anything just yet, all right?"

"All right," I concede.

***

Three hours later Detective Tucker is back.

"Your pal Bitzmore was holding out on me," he says tersely. "He now admits to placing an ad for a female voice-over artist. He hired her and had her read what he told her were excerpts from a thriller novel as an audition for making an audiobook. Then he ran those samples through the modulator and sent them to you. He paid her with a money order mailed to a P.O. box, and they only ever talked online."

"So that's it," I exclaim. "That's the last piece. We're clear."

"*No*," Allen stresses. "We still need to find out who hired Bitzmore, honey."

"If that part ever even happened in the first place. Bitzmore lied at first about any female accomplices," I point out. "What's to say he didn't lie about the rest of it, as well?"

"I intend to find out," Tucker promises us both. "I'll be in touch."

CHAPTER FIFTY-EIGHT
Allen

When a week passes, then two, with no more threatening messages to Brielle, I begin to breathe a little easier. It helps when Tucker's continued investigation seemingly contradicts the initial statements Bitzmore made during his first interview.

"Lone whackadoodle," he tells me over coffee. "Guy's got some serious mental issues and a very active imagination."

"Yeah," I agree, flexing the right shoulder that is still aching from the round of physical therapy earlier in the morning. "I wonder if his attorney will use that to try and plea bargain."

"I wouldn't be surprised at all," Tucker agrees. "Anyway, I thought you'd like to know where things stood."

***

I drive Brielle back over to her place right after lunch, and she is stunned – and not in a good way – to see over two hundred and fifty missed calls on her cell phone.

"It's going to take me forever to get caught up," she laments, and I go to her and take her in my arms.

"But you're still around to do it, and that's what matters," I tell her gently.

"I know," she says, and kisses me.

"Want to do dinner tonight?"

"Actually, I was thinking a girls' night in to celebrate," she tells me. "I know Mari's glad this is over, and poor Rita was beside herself with worry when she couldn't get a hold of me. I thought the three of us could sit around and have some wine and relax, maybe put on a movie."

"Besides," she says as she wraps her arms around my waist, "you could stand to put in some time at your office, you know."

"Yeah, I know," I admit, "but it's been nice having you all to myself these last two weeks."

She grins.

"I agree, but now we need to get back to reality."

"Call you later?"

"I'd like that."

I kiss her again before I retreat to my truck and head to the office.

CHAPTER FIFTY-NINE
Brielle

Both Mari and Rita sound excited about getting together, and I smile as I make my way to my home office.

It takes me four hours of non-stop work to whittle down the voicemails and put a sizeable dent in the well over three hundred emails that accumulated while I was in hiding.

Before I know it, my doorbell is chiming, and opening my front door reveals Mari standing there with a mischievous grin and a very familiar-looking box.

"Cheesecake?"

"You know it."

"You rock," I say and stand aside for her to enter.

We are just contemplating what to order for dinner when Rita shows up, brandishing a bottle of my favorite Moscato.

"Wow! My favorite wine, *and* cheesecake? I feel like I've hit the lottery," I say with a laugh, and hug Rita tightly then lead the way to the kitchen.

"I'm just happy you're okay, Brielle," Rita tells me, her face full of emotion. "I have to admit, I'm a little pissed that you didn't tell me what was going on so I could help."

"I know, Rita, and I'm sorry. But it was safer not to at the time. I hope you understand."

She smiles and nods. "I do. So, what's for dinner?"

"Hm," I say, biting my bottom lip, "what sounds better, Chinese, or pizza?"

The vote comes in unanimously for an extra-large pizza with pepperoni, mushrooms, and extra cheese, and I place the order.

"They said it will be here in about forty-five minutes," I announce.

"Good. Let's break open the wine, shall we?" Rita says as she uncorks the bottle. "Because it sounds like we have a lot to celebrate."

She pours three glasses, and we toast in my kitchen.

"Now then," I say as I lead the way into the living room, "we have a bunch of different movies to choose from. Any ideas?"

"Nothing violent," Mari says. "Keep it light."

"Ooh! Something romantic," Rita chimes in. "A rom-com is always good."

"Either of you ever seen *The Cutting Edge*?"

***

I move back to the kitchen to retrieve the bottle when my wineglass is empty.

"Anyone else need a refill?" I offer.

"Hit me," Mari says, and I dutifully pour.

"Rita, what about you?"

"Moscato's actually not my thing," she admits, "so I am just gonna nurse this one, then switch to iced tea."

"Fair enough," I say, top off my glass, and retake my seat on the left end of the couch.

I am about a third of the way through my second glass when my limbs begin to feel funny, like they are weighted down with lead. I turn my head to the right to look over at Mari and notice that she is pale, and her eyelids are drooping.

"Mari," I mumble, and my tongue feels thick. "Are you okay?"

"Don't... think so..." she croaks as her eyes roll back in her head.

The doorbell ringing sounds far, far away.

"Must be the pizza. I'll get it," Rita says, and jumps up to go to the door.

A few minutes later she is back.

"Pizza's here," she announces cheerfully as she holds up the box, "and I brought along a mutual friend of ours, as well."

She steps to one side and the menacing figure that moves forward into my swimming field of vision is none other than Tony, my psychotic ex.

Fear coils deep in my belly and I am frantic, trying to get to my feet, but my body is not cooperating very well, and I sag to the floor on my knees.

"You... you're supposed to be in prison in New York," I gasp, every muscle in my body weighing a ton.

"Enough money can accomplish anything," he snarls at me, and I blink rapidly when I notice that bone-deep crazy flashes like a strobe light in his brown eyes. "Including getting convictions overturned and altering computer records. I've been down here for six months now."

"How did you find me?"

He laughs, and a shiver runs down my spine.

"You told me all about dear old Aunt Betsy, remember? Wasn't hard to pick up your trail."

"What... happened... to your face..."

"This?" he gestures to the ragged scar that runs from his hairline down across his right cheek. "A gift from a cellmate. And that is just one of many that I owe you for, *Brielle*."

He tears his focus away from me long enough to scowl at Rita.

"I wanted her lucid for this. How much did you give her?"

"It's only her second glass, baby."

Baby? Did my assistant just call the most evil human being that I have ever met baby?

I do not realize I have spoken aloud until Tony is leaning over me, then dragging me to my feet.

"How about we go set that fancy alarm of yours, *Becka*," he growls, his face inches from mine, and I shudder at the sound of my old name passing his lips. "Wouldn't want anyone else to crash our party before it even gets started."

He marches me, staggering, to the front door and stations me in front of the panel.

"Set it," he demands.

My brain is swirling with whatever Rita drugged us with, and as I giggle uncontrollably Tony shakes then slaps me.

The memory of Pete familiarizing me with the setup surges to the forefront of my mind as I stretch my hand toward the keypad.

Remember, Brielle, this system has a panic feature. If you enter your code in backwards, the alarm will set – but it will also send a silent notification to us and the police. Okay?

Backwards, I echo in my fuzzy brain as I try like hell to remember my code. *One oh two two....*

My fingers fumble as I press two, two, zero, then one, then the pound sign. Immediately the alarm begins to chirp, and Tony smirks at me.

"Good," he leers as he drags me back toward the living room. "Now for the fun stuff."

"What's the matter?" Rita asks me with a strange smile on her face. "Can't hold your booze anymore?"

"Huh?"

"Or should I say it like this, so that it sounds more familiar..."

She clears her throat, pauses, then conjures up a dead-on imitation of the mysterious Midwestern caller who harassed me.

"What.... how..."

"You never bothered to get to know me, Brielle. I was just a servant to you," she snarls, her voice dripping with disdain. "Or what about this version..."

She clears her throat again, and the next time she speaks she sounds exactly like a middle-aged English man, followed by a raspy New York accent that is spot on.

"I can sound like anyone. I'm very gifted at it, actually, and it pays way better than schlepping for some snotty has-been who didn't know a good man when she had him."

I am dumbfounded.

"*Him*? You talking about *Tony*? Do you even know what he did to me?"

"I know enough to know you framed him for something he didn't do," she sneers, "because he told me all about it when we first met four months ago. Ain't that right, baby?"

I shake my head in disbelief, fighting to stay awake long enough to try to turn her into the ally that I thought she was.

"*Tony* is the guy you've been dating? Man, does he have you snowed. What did he promise you to get you to sell me out?"

"It's all about the ring, girlfriend," she says snidely, lifting her left hand and waving my old engagement ring, a huge princess-cut diamond, in my face. "And money. Lots and *lots* of money."

"Enough of this," Tony rasps, cutting Rita's confession short, then pins me against him and licks up the side of my neck as a fuming Rita glares at us. "How about I go introduce myself real good to your hot little friend over there? Or should I start with you?"

"Don't hurt Mari," I slur, my chin drooping. "Do what you want to me but leave her alone."

"That ain't the way this works, Becka, and you know it," he intones, grinding against me. "*I* call the shots here."

CHAPTER SIXTY
Allen

I take a break from catching up on my emails and head down the hall for another cup of coffee.

Eight-twenty, I note. *I'll stay just a little longer, then call it a night.*

I have just poured a fresh cup when I hear feet pounding down the hall and someone shouting my name.

"Allen!"

I stick my head out into the hallway.

"What?"

Sam stops short and whirls around to look at me.

"We gotta roll, boss. The panic code was entered at Brielle's place about forty seconds ago."

My coffee mug hits the floor and shatters.

We sprint out to the truck, and I peel out of the parking space and haul ass down the road, barking instructions that Sam passes along to the team on the walkie-talkies.

"Get Detective Tucker on the line," I tell him, then turn my focus completely toward making a usually ten-minute drive happen in less than half that time.

Hang in there, baby, I'm coming.

CHAPTER SIXTY-ONE
Brielle

Tony starts to manhandle me, sticking his tongue down my throat and groping my chest, when a horrible ominous *thunk* accompanied by glass breaking distracts him. He throws me to the ground and strides across the room to grab Rita by her hair.

"What did you do?" he demands.

"I heard what you just said," she fires back through clenched teeth. "And I am *not* just gonna stand by and watch you screw Mari or Brielle or anybody else, Tony. You're *my* man."

I can see Mari still slumped on the couch, and I stealthily crawl on all fours away from a yelling Tony and Rita, each movement heavy and hard, like my limbs weigh a thousand pounds apiece.

I reach Mari's side and only vaguely realize that I am kneeling in a pile of shattered glass. When I touch her hair, my hand comes away bloody, and in some deep recess of my brain it registers with me that Rita struck Mari over the head with the wine bottle in a fit of jealousy.

"Mari," I whisper, and clumsily pat her cheeks. "Mari, wake up."

Behind me I hear their argument crescendo into a frightened scream that cuts off abruptly, and I turn enough to see Rita clutching at her abdomen, her hands cupped tightly around the hilt of the knife that Tony just stabbed her with.

"The jealousy shit is getting old, babe. I think it's time we break up," he sneers, and laughs as he watches her stumble backward, then fall to the floor.

Gun in my purse, I finally remember through the drug-induced haze, and it gives me hope. *At the end of the couch!*

I begin to crawl again, hoping to God that Tony is still focused on Rita, and the bile rises in my throat when I realize that instead, he is closing in on a defenseless Mari with a predator's gleam.

"Unconscious works for me," he says, and the rage that builds in me helps me to stand.

I roar and stagger toward him, intent on defending the best friend I have ever had. But my equilibrium is still off, and Tony easily catches the right arm I try to punch him with and wrenches it behind my back. I scream as I feel and hear something ripping apart in my shoulder.

"Miss me that much, huh? Wait your turn," he growls. "Believe me, I'll be with you very soon. And then I will kill you both. But not before I make you watch me break in this hot little piece over here."

He releases my now dislocated arm and shoves me away, and I cry out as I land squarely on my injured right shoulder. The pain clears away the pharmaceutical fog and with an excruciating clarity I see it – my handbag with the gun in it, only about twelve inches away. I drag myself over, grab the gun, and release the safety, grateful that Allen insisted I keep a round chambered and ready to go.

Tony has just ripped open Mari's shirt when I get to my knees and shout, "Hey, asshole."

He turns and looks at me, amused.

"Whatever. You're not smart enough or brave enough to use that, Becka," he says in dismissal, then starts to turn back toward Mari.

I know what I have to do, and I call out to him again as I sight in left-handed.

When he sighs, stands upright, and turns to face me a second time, I open fire, just as Allen taught me, and I keep shooting until the clip is empty.

Tony staggers back, eyes wide with surprise, mouth gaping open and working soundlessly, then looks down at his chest where a crimson fountain spews forth.

"You... bitch..." he wheezes before he falls backward, crashing through my coffee table.

Another loud crash has me swiveling my head, then dropping the gun and reaching out my good arm toward Allen, who has skidded to a stop on his knees beside me and is hugging me tightly.

"Oh, thank God, thank God," I hear him say repeatedly as he kisses my forehead, cheeks, lips, hair.

"Hi, honey. Mari's hurt," is all I can force out before I faint.

CHAPTER SIXTY-TWO
Allen

I wait by her bedside, clasping her left hand tightly, anxious for her to wake and look at me.

Bastard tore her rotator cuff all to hell, I remember the surgeon telling me, and I growl.

And she offed his ass. He deserved it. It was very satisfying when they told me he was pronounced dead at the scene.

Brielle shudders, then moans, a haunted, wounded sound that breaks my heart all over again and takes me right back to the abject terror I felt as we raced to her house.

A light knock on the doorframe, and I glance over.

"Hey, Sam."

"How is she?" he asks.

"Still sleeping off the anesthesia," I tell him. "How are the other two doing?"

"Her assistant is still in surgery," he reveals. "And Tucker was just telling me that Mari's got a skull fracture and swelling on the brain. They're keeping her in a medically induced coma for the next forty-eight hours to give her body a chance to fight the swelling on its own."

I wince.

"What the hell happened tonight?" I wonder aloud.

"We can play back the tape," Sam says, and I look at him, confused.

"Didn't Pete tell you? Another thing about that system's panic feature is that when it is activated, it also prompts all interior cameras to record. Audio *and* video. It is a brand-new customization that Pete came up with. Brielle's place was the beta test for it."

"I want it. *Now*."

"Pete already collected it all, boss, and he said to tell you he can queue it up the moment you get back to the office."

"Nope," I say. "I'm not leaving her. I will watch it here."

"On it, boss."

***

A half-hour later my team has assembled. I have Pete's laptop balanced across my knees and am putting earbuds in so I can hear the audio without disturbing Brielle.

I take a deep breath, brace myself, and press 'play'. Immediately I am thrown into the nightmare that the love of my life and her best friend endured – starting with Rita's betrayal.

The split screen enables me to see both Tony's lecherous assault on Brielle and Rita's attack on Mari at once, and I shake with barely controlled rage.

It gets worse as the video progresses and I watch Brielle's ex argue with then stab Rita, and I snarl when I hear him boldly announce his intention to rape and kill Mari and Brielle.

I fight back nausea and stay the course, proud as hell when I watch Brielle take aim and fire, then relieved to see myself come barreling through the front door and racing over to hold her. Around us, my team and armed police officers fan out across the screen to check Mari, Rita, and the sadistic bastard taking his last pitiful, painful breath on the living room floor.

Tucker's face is agonized when he crouches down beside Mari, then suddenly scoops her up and rushes for the front door. I did not notice it in the chaos of real time, but it is as plain as day in the playback, and it breaks my heart to witness.

My team watches me quietly as I reach up with shaking hands and take the earbuds out, and it takes me a few minutes to rein my seething fury in enough to speak.

"Make a copy of this, and make sure Tucker gets it," I tell Pete. "If she survives, that bitch Rita is going to jail for a long, long time."

I hand Pete's laptop back to him, and one by one they file out, each of them shaking my hand or squeezing my good shoulder in a show of solidarity.

The last to leave is Hope, who leans down and whispers, "By the way, I almost forgot to tell you — Brielle's favorite color is royal blue," before she too pats my shoulder and walks out the door.

EPILOGUE
Allen

"When people talk about 'couples' therapy', I don't think this is what they mean," Brielle says with a grin as we walk into the physical therapy center side-by-side four weeks later.

"Look at it this way. We're bonding, right?" I offer hopefully, and chuckle when she rolls her eyes at me.

"Sure. Bonding," she answers, then leans in to give me a kiss. "But you're doing better at it than I am."

"Well, I did have a two-week head start on you, you know," I remind her. "You'll get there."

"Here's hoping."

***

The following afternoon we get confirmation that Rita, who survived her injuries, has been indicted on multiple charges – including attempted murder for her attack on Mari - and will stand trial, as will ex-realtor Scott Bitzmore for his involvement in the plot.

Brielle is determined to testify if needed, but I assure her that the evidence Tucker has already gathered – including the security system recording – should be plentiful enough to put Rita and Bitzmore both away for a long time.

***

Two days later, we are lounging in bed on a lazy Sunday morning, and Brielle turns to me.

"I don't want to live in that house anymore," she says softly against my chest as she snuggles closer. "I want to sell it and move in here."

"Fine by me," I say, gently stroking up and down her back. "On one condition."

She lifts her head and looks at me, completely stunned.

"Condition? What condition?"

I roll away from her long enough to retrieve the small velvet ring box from my nightstand and open it before I turn to face her again.

"On the condition that you say you'll marry me, because I am head over heels in love with you, Brielle," I say, and show her the dainty silver, diamond, and sapphire engagement ring that I had custom-made just for her.

Her eyes fill with tears and her bottom lip trembles before she takes a deep breath and whispers, "I love you too, Allen. Yes, I will marry you."

I slide the ring onto her finger, toss the box out of our way, then carefully slide her warm, soft body up and onto mine, knowing to my core that Brielle is not the only one who was saved.

"Welcome home, baby," I whisper before I kiss her.

***

Author's Notes, Part One:

First, I really hope you enjoyed "Saving Brielle" and meeting all of Allen's team members! Seven books are planned in the series, and while they will each be completely captivating as standalones, they will be much more fun if read in order.

"Minding Mari", the continuation of Tucker and Mari's story, will be out sometime in early 2023, and you can stay up to date on the latest release news by visiting my website and other places I hang out. The 'blurb' for Minding Mari is below!

Minding Mari: Love's Defender – Book Two

<u>Mari Blaylock</u>– *The once bubbly and vivacious free-spirited photographer who is struggling to regain her footing after a horrific attack robs her of part of her memories – and her sense of security.*

<u>Adam Tucker</u> – *The jaded detective who's attracted to Mari the first time he meets her.*

When a photograph Mari does not even remember taking puts her in the crosshairs of some ruthless people, Adam must protect her at all costs – even if it means sacrificing everything, including his life.

Links below:

Faith's *Love's Defender* series page

Faith's BOOKBUB Profile

Faith's GOODREADS Profile

Follow me on Facebook!

Wanna read more? Try one of my romance novellas – FREE – Just click here.

Like a good mystery/thriller? I write those as D.F. Hart – and book one in my Vital Secrets series is FREE. Click here to get your copy and check it out.

Lastly, the best gift an author can receive is honest feedback about their work. If you could take a moment and leave a review on your favorite retailer and other places, such as Bookbub and Goodreads, it would mean the world to me.

Author's Notes, Part Two:

Erin Wright and **Paul Austin Ardoin** are absolutely real - and absolutely riveting - writers, and if you would like to check out their works you can do so by clicking the following links:

Go to ERIN's site

Go to PAUL's site

www.ingramcontent.com/pod-product-compliance
Lightning Source LLC
Chambersburg PA
CBHW020320260626

47156CB00004B/1309